MURDER
TAKES
ALL

Book Four In The
O'Toole/Starker
Murder Mystery Series

G. A. Cockerham

This is a work of fiction. Names, characters, businesses, places, events and incidents are either the products of the author's imagination or used in a fictitious manner. Any resemblance to actual persons, living or dead, or actual events is purely coincidental.

ISBN-13: 978-1-7339973-2-4

Also by G. A. Cockerham

O'TOOLE/STARKER
OREGON COAST MURDER MYSTERIES

Murder On The Oregon Coast

Murder On The Wind

Murder Replete...*for now*

Featured in Fall 2019 issue of *Southern Oregon* Magazine
Who's Who, What's What Book Picks.

Acknowledgements

I've listed below several people whose expertise contributed greatly to the human-interest aspects of my mystery, providing input based upon personal experience. To each I give my gratitude.

My husband, Bruce Cockerham, edits my law enforcement references and is my constant source of support and encouragement. He is a retired police captain with thirty years of experience in law enforcement. He's worked in patrol, traffic, detectives, SWAT, administration, and as an academy instructor. Bruce trained with the FBI as a counter sniper and is a graduate of both the California Command College and the FBI Academy. He holds a BA from Whitworth University and an MDiv from the San Francisco Theological Seminary.

Forensic DNA expert Camilla Green gives me great ideas on little-known forensic techniques. Cami's suggestions add a dose of excitement for me as well as my readers.

Joshua Teter started his seven-year career in Nye County, Nevada, and is currently assigned to the Patrol – K-9 unit for the Curry County Sheriff's Office. Deputy Teter and his drug dog Axel have proven to be great assets for the sheriff.

Gail Whitmore has been Office Manager for the Gold Beach, Oregon Police Department for fifteen years. In 2008 she was certified by the State and sworn in by the DA as Deputy Medical Examiner for Gold Beach.

TABLE OF CONTENTS

Acknowledgements   v

Chapter One   1

Chapter Two   9

Chapter Three   19

Chapter Four   25

Chapter Five   29

Chapter Six   39

Chapter Seven   43

Chapter Eight   49

Chapter Nine   53

Chapter Ten   61

Chapter Eleven   69

Chapter Twelve   75

Chapter Thirteen   85

Chapter Fourteen   95

Chapter Fifteen   105

Chapter Sixteen   109

Chapter Seventeen   115

Chapter Eighteen   119

Chapter Nineteen   127

Chapter Twenty   135

Chapter Twenty-One   141

Chapter Twenty-Two   149

Chapter Twenty-Three   157

Chapter Twenty-Four   163

Chapter Twenty-Five   171

Chapter Twenty-Six   179

Chapter Twenty-Seven   183

Chapter Twenty-Eight   189

Chapter Twenty-Nine   197

Chapter Thirty   205

Epilogue   213

CHAPTER ONE

The room was small, about ten by fifteen feet. Having been closed up tight, it had a cold dampness, and the darkness held no glimmer of light. Moving boxes were stacked, taking up half of the floor space. A man's bicycle leaned against one side wall. Along the opposite wall were stored several items including a large stainless-steel pot, a temperature gauge, some coiled copper tubing with a plastic fitting at one end, a long plastic spoon, several white buckets, and a bottle of bleach. There were a few smaller items lying on top of the pots. This left about a five-by-five-foot space on which nothing had been stored, but it wasn't empty. A woman lay face up and a man face down. Their otherwise perfect repose was marred only by the gunshot wounds: her two in the chest and his one in the head.

Outside the room a man put his key in the lock and lifted the roll-up door.

* * *

It was a typical July morning for the southern Oregon coast. The temperature was sixty-two degrees, and visibility was about two hundred feet through the fog, which was as thick as the chowder for which many coastal towns are known. Detectives Patty O'Toole and Rick Starker sat at their desks, each with a mug of hot coffee and a pastry. Rick's penchant for bacon-topped maple bars was well known in the small department, but a pastry of any kind was acceptable when he couldn't find his favorite. Patty hadn't eaten many doughnuts before Rick had arrived, but over time she too had acquired a taste for something sweet with her morning coffee.

Patty set her coffee cup down, looked around their office space, and asked Rick, "How long have we worked together in this office?"

Rick looked up from his notes. "I left Boston for Brookings about seven years ago. Why do you ask?"

"I'm just noticing how bare the walls are. It's not very warm in here."

Without looking up, Rick responded, "It's an office. And the temperature's fine with me."

Patty smiled. "I wasn't referring to the temperature. I mean that the stark walls don't evoke a warm feeling. Has it never crossed your mind that this room needs something more?"

Rick now looked up. "Something more? I have a desk and a phone. What else do I need?"

Patty looked around the room. "Oh, I don't know. Maybe one or two nice paintings so that we have something to look at other than the tops of our desks and paperwork."

"We do have something to look at," Rick said. "We have a window with a view that does, at times…" He paused, furrowed his eyebrows and pursed his lips as though thinking of what he wanted to say. "That does at times evoke deep feelings in me." Patty started to protest. Rick held up the palm of his hand toward her so that she'd let him continue. "At other times the view is educational. Currently, it's telling me that the fog has dampened the concrete parking lot and that I can't see any further now than I did when I came to work. If I look out again in thirty minutes, it may tell me that the sun's rays have broken through and the temperature is ten degrees warmer."

Patty looked out the window as Rick spoke. "Did you have a window in your Boston office?"

"I don't remember a window, but then I'm not sure I ever paid attention to the office walls. My head was always down, reviewing cases or writing reports."

Patty and Rick looked into each other's eyes. "Okay," she said. "I just thought that a painting or two would be nice in here."

"Patty, if you want to put paintings on the walls, go ahead and put them up."

"So you wouldn't mind or feel like I was interfering with your space?"

Rick smiled. "Not at all. We've got a window."

The radio on Patty's desk crackled, and dispatch relayed a call with possible fatalities. Officer Burt (Brad) Bradley responded that he was on his way. Immediately after Brad's call, Officer Pete Chekowsky informed dispatch that he too was en route.

Ten minutes later, Patty's phone rang, and she set the half-eaten doughnut back into the white pastry bag. "Where? Any witnesses? Who called it in? You got a phone number and address? Okay. Tape off the perimeter and tell the manager to close the place down. No one goes in or out unless authorized. Rick and I are on our way. You call Kindle. I'll call the ME after we've taken a look."

Rick popped the last bite of his pastry into his mouth, took a quick sip of coffee, felt with the inside of his arm that his gun was holstered, and grabbed his jacket as they left the room. "Must be that fatalities are confirmed if you've need for the medical examiner."

"They are. At the Seaside Storage Facility. Brad's already there. Let's take your car, and I'll fill you in on the way."

Upon arriving at the scene, the detectives found Officer Chekowsky using crime-scene tape to rope off a row of storage units. Officer Bradley was talking to a middle-aged man. A younger man stood by himself, leaning against the door of the adjacent storage shed.

The detectives opened the trunk of their unmarked car, and each took out a pair of crime-scene booties, coveralls, and a pair of nitrile gloves. Rick picked up his camera and put the strap around his neck before they both walked over to the open unit.

"Hey, Brad, what have we got?" Patty asked.

Brad walked away from the man he was talking with and gave his attention to the detectives. "Two bodies," he said. "By the smell and the looks of

3

them, I'd guess they've been in there awhile. There's a gun in what's left of the male's hand suggesting a murder-suicide." Brad then pointed toward the man standing by himself outside of the unit. "He's the tenant. I was just talking with the facility manager. He and his wife own the place. I've got contact information for all of them."

Patty walked into the unit and stood still, taking in the scene as her eyes adjusted to the darkness. Rick walked up and turned to speak to her. He paused as he noticed the puzzled expression on his partner's face.

"That seems unusual," she said, pointing to the gun lying next to the male's hand. "In a suicide with gunshot to the head, recoil often carries the weapon out of the shooter's hand. It appears that he still had his index finger engaged with the trigger after the shot."

"I agree," said Rick. "I'll take the photos we need, including a couple close-ups of his hand."

"That's good," said Patty as she looked at her initial notes. "Brad briefly spoke with the tenant, a Gerold Dorisko. Let's find out what he knows."

Upon approaching the tenant, Patty showed her identification. "Mr. Dorisko, we're Detectives O'Toole and Starker. We understand you've been leasing this storage unit."

"I have, for about ten months. This is horrible! Will the police have my unit cleaned?"

"Not the police," said Patty. "You'll need to talk with your insurance company."

Patty continued asking questions while Rick wrote on his small notepad. "When did you arrive today?" she asked.

The tenant looked at his watch. "About nine."

"And when did you discover the deceased?"

"When I rolled up the door."

"Do you open your unit every day?" Patty asked.

"No. It's been about two months. I opened it this morning because I wanted to get my bike."

"You don't ride your bike regularly?"

"No, at least I haven't for the past several months."

"Why today?"

"I dunno. I just got up this morning and thought it'd be nice to take a bike ride."

Rick looked closely at the lock without touching it. "We'll have this lock processed for prints and examined for damage or tool marks, but it doesn't look tampered with at all from what I can see. Who else has a key to this unit?"

"No one," said the tenant.

Patty paused and then looked Dorisko in the eyes. "Did you know either of the deceased?"

Dorisko looked at Patty and shook his head. "How am I supposed to answer that? It's hard to tell what they looked like."

"Any idea why there'd be two bodies in your storage unit?"

The man shook his head again. "No."

"This is quite a mystery, Mr. Dorisko," Patty said. "You say that the unit was locked and that you're the only one with a key to the lock. The lock does not look like it's been tampered with, and you don't know why there are two bodies on the floor of your unit. So how do you think they got there?"

"I don't know," he said. "I keep the unit locked."

Patty continued to look closely at Dorisko. "So tell me again: how many people have keys to your lock?"

"Just me," he said before an extended pause.

Patty and Rick stood quietly as Dorisko stared at the ground before looking up again. "I just remembered. My brother has a key."

Patty and Rick looked at each other. Then Patty asked, "Your brother?"

"Yeah, I forgot until just now that I'd given him a key about six months ago so that he could store some of his stuff in here."

Rick, with pen in hand, said, "We need your brother's name and contact information."

Dorisko suddenly became a bit animated, rubbing his hand across his forehead and shifting from one foot to the next. "He doesn't have anything to do with this. He lives two hundred miles away in Eugene and hasn't been here since leaving his stuff."

"We still need his name and contact information," Rick said.

The nervous-looking man seemed to plead with Patty. "Look, my brother's been in some trouble in the past, and he's really been working hard to stay on the right side of the law. I'm begging you, please don't drag him into this. It could really set him back."

"What kind of trouble?" Patty asked.

"What?" asked Dorisko.

"You said your brother's been in trouble. What kind of trouble?"

Patty and Rick watched as the tenant, visibly uncomfortable, shifted his body weight.

"He got into trouble with drugs. His so-called buddy got him started and then involved him in some crimes. He spent four months in prison. That's why he needed to store his stuff in my shed. He's been out about two months and is trying hard to stay clean. Please don't hassle him about this. I'm sure he doesn't know any more than I do."

"What's his name?" Patty asked.

"David Dorisko."

"And his phone number and address?" Rick asked.

"All I have is his phone number. He doesn't have an address as far as I know. Moves around a lot, staying with friends."

"When's the last time you spoke with your brother?" Patty asked.

"Not for months," he said.

Patty stared into his eyes. "Then how do you know how well he's doing?"

With arms folded across his chest, Dorisko looked straight ahead into the distance as if that was going to save him from having to answer the question. "I spoke with my brother about two weeks ago. He said he was doing great and would come out to see me soon."

Patty pointed to a car parked just beyond Dorisko's unit. "That your car?"

"Yes."

"Mind if we take a look inside?"

"I guess not."

Patty checked out the front and back seats while Rick opened the trunk. He took a thorough look, closed it up, and walked over to Patty. "Nothing," he said.

"Same here," said Patty.

They walked back to talk with the tenant.

"Okay, Mr. Dorisko," Patty said. "Do you have any vacation plans in the near future?"

Dorisko shook his head. "No. Why?"

"We'd like to be able to contact you if we have additional questions."

The man looked back into the storage unit and then at Patty. "What do I do about them?"

"You're not going to do anything about them. And you can't enter your unit again or access your belongings until we've completed our investigation."

"What? I can't even get my bike? Why?"

"Because this is a crime scene, and until we're done with our investigation, your unit and everything in it are part of our crime scene. We'll be securing the door with one of our locks. You'll get yours back when we're done."

"How long will this take?" he asked, pacing back and forth.

"I can't tell you that right now."

With frustration building up, the young man turned around and began to walk back to his car.

"Excuse me, Mr. Dorisko," Patty said before he got far. "Does your brother own a firearm?"

"Not that I know of," he said, turning to Patty. "I've told you everything I know."

"Okay, but you'll need to remain here until the DME comes. He may want to talk with you."

"DME?" he asked.

"Deputy Medical Examiner."

The storage facility manager approached Patty and Rick. "Do you need me for anything?" he asked.

"You're the manager?" Patty asked.

"Yes. My name's Lawrence Smiter. My wife and I own the place."

"We have a couple of questions," Patty said. "Do you live here on site?"

"We live in the small house up front, next to the entrance."

"When did you learn about the deceased individuals?"

"My tenant ran up here and told me right after he called the police. I told him to stay outside of his unit."

"Have you seen anyone other than Gerold Dorisko going in or out of his storage unit?"

"Other than when he moved in, I haven't seen anyone going into his unit. My wife and I both have part-time jobs, though, so one or the other of us is not here for several hours during the day."

"Do you remember hearing anything like a gunshot about a month ago?"

"No, but then my wife and I both wear ear plugs. We both snore."

Rick looked down the driveway between the two rows of units. "Looks like there are a few surveillance cameras on the property. We'll need to look at the recorded images."

"Well, I can't help you there. I quit charging the batteries a couple years ago. They were taking photos twenty to thirty times a night. The bats and critters on the roofs were constantly triggering the cameras."

Rick and Patty looked at each other before Rick wrote down the response.

Pete walked up before Patty could ask another question. "Ted Kindle's tied up with a death in Langlois, so he's asked Gwen Holland to help out."

"Thanks, Pete," Patty said. She then turned her attention back to Smiter. "That's all we have for now. Detective Starker here will take down your phone number. We'll be in touch if we have more questions."

CHAPTER TWO

The Gold Beach Deputy Medical Examiner, Gwen Holland, pulled up to the scene. She stepped out of her car, put on her white jumpsuit, pulled cloth booties over her shoes, and slipped her hands into nitrile gloves.

"Glad you could make it, Gwen," Patty called out. "Ted let us know that we'd have the pleasure of working with you on this. How are things in Gold Beach?"

"No real problems," she said, "but I understand you've got two. Any idea how long they've been here?"

"Hard to tell in their mummified state. The tenant says he hasn't opened his unit in two months. We'll have to wait for Doc Miller to give us an estimated time of death."

Gwen smiled. "So, what you're telling me is that I'm here solely due to protocol."

Rick quickly spoke up. "Never, Gwen. We always appreciate your and Ted's opinions, regardless of any other factors."

"Thanks, Rick. I was beginning to feel like I wasn't needed."

The two detectives and Gwen walked into the storage unit, and Patty asked, "Have you seen anything like this before?"

"A few years ago," Gwen said. "The deceased had been missing for several weeks when he was found. He was a little further along, however, and was entering the skeletonization process. You've probably taken photos, Rick, but I always like to take my own. One of us may catch something the other didn't." Gwen looked at Patty. "Before we continue, you might want to call the ME. I think she's going to want to fly out here as soon as possible. These two aren't going to transfer well when we move them into a hearse."

Patty nodded. "Give me a minute," she said before stepping out of the unit.

Patty made her call and returned. "You're right. The doc will be here in about an hour. Do you want to wait for her before turning the bodies or do you want to inspect them now?"

"Let's wait for the doc," said Gwen. "I'll use the time to make a scene sketch for my report. I'd also like to talk with the tenant."

Forty minutes later, Gwen Holland had completed her sketch and her interview with Gerold Dorisko. She began taking photos of the scene. "I'm taking several of his hand and the gun. I'd say someone staged this to look like a suicide. It makes no sense that his finger would still be around the trigger if he shot himself."

Patty and Rick exchanged glances. "That's what we think," said Patty.

"You'll want confirmation from the ME, but it appears as though it was the gunshots that killed them. In my opinion, you have a double homicide. I'll be interested in learning what the doc says."

"I've got a question for you, Gwen," Patty said. "How far away would you estimate the gun was when he was shot?"

"Well, the ballistic experts will answer that, but I'd guess five to eight feet, judging from the powder tattooing or stippling, blood spatter, and damage to his skull."

Patty nodded. "More reasons for this not to be a suicide."

Officer Bradley pulled up with the Jackson County Medical Examiner, Doctor Miller. She also put on a suit, booties, and gloves before joining the detectives and DME.

"Hey, Doc," said Patty. "Thanks for coming out on such short notice."

"Hi, Patty." The doc then looked toward Rick. "How are you, Rick?"

"Doing well, Doc. And you?"

The doctor smiled. "Busier than ever, but then I'm told that's job security, so I don't complain." She then gave her attention to the DME. "It's been a while since I've seen you, Gwen. Not busy enough in Gold Beach so you're taking over Ted's territory?"

Gwen laughed. "You've got me pegged," she said. "I'm glad you could make it out as we don't think the bodies will transfer very well."

"Did you get your photos?"

"I did," said Gwen.

"Well, I won't need to duplicate yours if you'll send them to me."

"Sure thing, Doc."

"Rick, can I ask you to be ready with the camera when Gwen and I turn the bodies?"

"Just let me know when to shoot," he said, to which the three women all chuckled. Rick smiled. "No pun intended."

The doc made a cursory view of the bodies. "Call the funeral home, Patty, and ask them to send a driver as soon as possible. I'd like to be here when the bodies are moved. Tell them that the bodies are mummified and that we'll need to move them onto a cadaver carrier that can be placed directly in the cold chambers overnight, then used to transport the bodies to my lab tomorrow."

Patty stepped out again for a few minutes. After talking with the funeral home receptionist, she joined the others. "The hearse should be here in about twenty minutes, Doc. They'll have what you requested."

"Now, Gwen," said Doc, "it's not often I get to work the scene with a DME. After taking your photos, what's the next thing you'd do before moving the bodies?"

Gwen smiled. "Before I moved the male, I'd remove the firearm, take out any unspent ammunition, and photograph it all."

Now it was the doc's turn to smile. "I'll wait."

Gwen removed the gun and took her photos. She then placed the gun in an evidence bag, labeled it PIC, and signed her name. She added the firearm on the PIC form as evidence.

"The Property In Custody process," said the doc, "can be one of the most important things you do, both for the safety of those around you and for court evidence. Good work! Now let's turn him over."

When the doc and Gwen turned the male, they all noticed a small metal object that had been hidden by the body. "A .45 casing," said the doc. "This suggests that she was shot first if the 1911 in his hand was used to kill her. We'll need a photo of this, Rick, before you pick it up."

"Finding the casing also suggests," said Patty, "that the shooter is not knowledgeable enough to know to pick up the casings."

"Or just plain sloppy," said Gwen.

Patty nodded. "We'll get a warrant to search for the others."

Gwen and the doc repeated the process with the female.

"No signs of trauma other than the gunshot wounds on either of them," said the doc. She looked at Patty. "You find anything to identify them?"

"Nothing at all, and the mummified state of the fingers means we can't use prints. It's going to require a more time-consuming investigation."

Doc Miller looked up at Patty. "But not impossible," she said.

Thirty minutes later, the doc had finished her initial exam of the bodies. "I'm not going to make any guesstimates here," she said. "Give me a couple of days in my lab and I'll be able to tell you time of death and confirm how they died." She gave instructions to the hearse driver, and he and Rick were able to move the bodies onto the carriers and into the hearse. When the transfer was complete, Brad lowered the storage unit door and put the new lock on it.

"Do you have time for lunch?" Patty asked.

"I appreciate the invitation, but no. I left in the middle of an autopsy to come over here. I need to get back and finish up today."

"I'll ask Pete to take you back to the airport," said Patty. "We sure appreciate your help on this. A double homicide out here is pretty rare, and the stage of decomposition of our victims was also a first for me and Rick."

"Well," said the doc, "you'll both be more informed next time. Give me a call in a couple of days if I haven't first called you."

Officer Chekowsky left to take the doc to the airport.

Patty looked at Gwen. "How about you, Gwen? Do you have time for lunch?"

"Lunch would be great," said Gwen, "and I'd like to go to Blue Water if that works for both of you. I haven't eaten yet, and they serve breakfast all day."

"Works for me," said Rick. "I think I've tried most items on the menu and it's all good."

"I've been told that everything is homemade," said Patty. "Their Caesar Salad dressing is the best I've tasted. And about Blue Water, did either of you know that a group of retired cops meets there every month?"

"I didn't," said Rick.

"I've heard a little about the group," said Gwen. "The retirees are from various agencies throughout the country. I've heard there are guys from city, county, and federal agencies."

"Not just guys," said Patty. "There's at least one female, and her law enforcement career was spent in two states. I hope they're still active when I retire."

"That's asking a lot of those folks, Patty," Rick said with a smile. "Some are already in their late seventies and early eighties, and you've got at least another twenty-something years."

Patty looked at Gwen and slowly shook her head. "See what I have to put up with?"

"Let's go to lunch," said Gwen.

"On the way," said Patty, "I'll call dispatch and ask for a background check on David Dorisko. I need to know if he has a parole officer before we get in touch with him."

The detectives and Gwen were shown to a table where they ordered and enjoyed coffee while waiting for their food.

"The doc sure stays busy," said Rick.

Gwen agreed. "She does. As the only state medical examiner for five counties, including two in California, I expect she never has a free moment."

"You know, Gwen, though we've known each other for about fifteen years, I've never asked about your role as a Deputy ME. What got you interested in the position?"

"I've worked around law enforcement for a long time, and a friend suggested I'd be good at this. I thought it might be interesting and decided to take the training. Turns out that it's very interesting."

Rick poured cream into his coffee. "How and where did you train?"

"I was required to take a forty-hour course in Clackamas County. The training was great and included many types of calls. We went over the history of DMEs and dabbled in pathology. Following the course, I completed an externship with a pathologist."

"Any continuing ed?" asked Rick.

"Twelve hours of training per year is required to maintain my certification with the state."

"Sounds interesting," said Patty. "I know from experience that you don't go on calls if the deceased has died under the care of Hospice or has spent less than twenty-four hours in a hospital under a doctor's care. Are there any other circumstances that would not require your assistance?"

Gwen nodded. "If I show up and learn it's an assisted suicide, I immediately leave."

"When we work with Ted," Rick said, "he won't leave the body until it's turned over to the funeral home. Is this true for you too?"

"It's how we work. Sort of like the chain-of-evidence rules. I want to know that nothing has happened to the body between my examination and receipt by the funeral home."

"Do you follow up with the ME to confirm cause of death?" Rick asked.

"Absolutely. I want to know if I got it right and to learn if the circumstances of death were unclear, or if I missed something."

Patty smiled. "It's great that you can do this while also holding down a full-time job."

"That's due to the size of the population in Gold Beach. I'm sure that there are others in highly-populated areas who are employed full time as a DME."

The detectives and Gwen finished up their lunches, and Gwen left on her return trip to Gold Beach. Patty and Rick drove back to their office where they each found their phone message lights blinking. Patty listened to a couple of messages, jotted down a few notes and hung up the phone. She waited for Rick to finish writing before filling him in on the content of one call. "David Dorisko is on parole and has a Lane County PO. I'll call and let her know what's up before we contact him. But first I'll update the LT."

The lieutenant's office was down the hall.

"Come in, O'Toole. Tell me about the call."

Patty explained what they'd found and went over the findings of Doc Miller and Gwen Holland.

"A double homicide," said the lieutenant. "Rick investigated a lot of murders during his years in Boston and came to us with a great record. The two of you should be able to handle this."

"I'm sure we can, LT. Thank you."

Patty returned to her desk and filled Rick in on her conversation with the lieutenant.

"Do you have time tomorrow to drive to Eugene and meet with David Dorisko?"

Rick looked at his calendar. "I've got court in the morning, but it shouldn't take long. I expect to be done by nine-thirty. You can pick me up at the courthouse, so set the appointment up for two. That will give us time for a quick lunch before the meeting."

"Okay," Patty said. "We'll have an hour for the appointment and can still get back to Brookings by seven-thirty or so. I'll call our sheriff and then David's PO. Would you request a warrant to search the storage unit?"

"Sure," said Rick. "Anything other than the contents you want the warrant to cover?"

"Request it for the unit, Gerold's phone, house, and computer." Patty tapped the sheriff's number into her phone and heard him pick up after two rings.

"Hello, Detective," he said.

"Hey, Sheriff. How's your day going?"

"Better than yours. Heard you've got a couple of bodies. Any ID?"

"None," said Patty. "Looks like a double homicide, though someone staged it to look like a murder/suicide. The tenant renting the storage unit lives in Harbor. We may need your help on this one."

"Let me know what you need."

"Thanks, Sheriff. I'll keep you posted if this turns into something much larger than it appears."

"We've now got a great canine unit if you think drugs are involved."

"I heard. Congratulations! I'd like to see them in action, and this might be the incident for it. Drugs could be involved, though we don't know yet what's stored in the unit. I just know it's not as simple as it was meant to appear. Do you think that one of your deputies and a drug dog could drop by the crime scene tomorrow?"

"Best if you give him a call direct," said the sheriff. "His name's Jake Browning."

Patty jotted down the deputy's name and phone number. "Thanks, Sheriff. I'll give Jake a call."

Before calling the deputy, Patty tapped in the number of David Dorisko's PO.

A woman answered the call. "Deputy Lincoln."

Patty introduced herself. "We've had a double shooting out here, and you're the PO for someone in Eugene we need to interview."

"What's the name, Detective?"

"David Dorisko."

"David just got out of prison. I'm sorry to learn he's already in trouble again."

"He's not a suspect yet," said Patty.

"But he is a person of interest," said the deputy.

"Yes," said Patty. "He holds one of two keys to his brother's storage unit, where two bodies have been found."

"Drugs involved?" asked Lincoln.

"The deaths are suspicious," Patty said, "but the involvement of drugs has not yet been confirmed."

"I have no problem with your seeing him, but I would like to know when and where."

"I'll let you know once I've confirmed it with Dorisko. We'd prefer someplace other than the PD."

"No Miranda requirement," said Lincoln.

"It helps," said Patty.

"Understood," said Lincoln. "I'll need to be kept abreast if you find he's involved."

"We'll do that."

Patty placed the call to David using the number his brother had provided. After two rings a man answered. "Hello."

"David Dorisko?" Patty asked.

"Who's this?"

"This is Detective O'Toole with the Brookings Police Department. Your brother Gerold gave me your phone number."

"Okay," he said. "What do you want?"

"Earlier today, two people were found dead in your brother's storage unit. He says you have a key to the roll-up door. That gives you access, and we need to talk with you. My partner and I can meet you in Eugene, or you can come to Brookings."

"Look. I don't even know where my key is. I haven't needed to get in since we stored my stuff months ago."

"I can appreciate that, Mr. Dorisko, but we need to talk with you. Do you want us to meet you in Eugene tomorrow, or do you want to come here to our office?"

"This is unreal," he said. After a brief pause, he continued, "I don't have a car, so you'll have to come here. You can meet me at the McDonald's at West Sixth."

"We can do that," said Patty. "Let's make it at two."

"Okay," he said.

"Do you have something you can write with? I want you to call me before eight tomorrow morning if for any reason you can't keep the meeting."

"Yeah. Okay. Give me the number."

Patty read off her cell phone number and requested that it be read back to her. "So we'll see you tomorrow afternoon at McDonald's," she said.

After finishing the call, Patty made note of the time and location in her phone calendar.

When she looked up, Rick was walking into the office with a plate of cookies.

"Want one?" he asked as Patty watched him place the paper plate on the side of his desk.

"Maybe tomorrow morning with coffee if there are any left," she said.

"Well, I expect there will be unless something unforeseen happens and I have to work late."

Patty smiled. "David Dorisko will meet us tomorrow in Eugene."

CHAPTER THREE

The next day Patty picked Rick up at the courthouse, and they proceeded up the Oregon coast to Highway 126, where they'd turn off for Eugene and their appointment with David Dorisko.

"What do you know about Port Orford?" Patty asked.

Rick turned toward Patty. "I know it's about thirty minutes north of Gold Beach and about the same south of Bandon."

"Is that all?" Patty asked.

"It is, though I think I'm about to learn more."

"Port Orford," Patty began, "is the westernmost city in the contiguous US. Washington has a few unincorporated areas that are further northwest, but Port Orford has that position among cities."

"That accounts," Rick said, "for the increased mile-per-hour wind speed they have over Brookings."

"It does," Patty said.

"What else?" Rick asked.

"Well," said Patty, "ever heard of the State of Jefferson?"

"Sure. It's comprised of several counties in northern California that want to secede from the state of California and become our fifty-first state."

"Did you know," asked Patty, "that the first reference to the State of Jefferson was right here in Port Orford?"

"I didn't," said Rick. "How did it start?"

"In 1941 the mayor of Port Orford became frustrated with how the poor highway conditions hampered economic development in his town. So he suggested that a number of counties along the Oregon and California coast should secede and create their own state called Jefferson."

"That's interesting," said Rick. "But clearly they didn't succeed. Do you know why?"

"The movement came to an end when Pearl Harbor was bombed, and the US became involved in World War II. It has, however, in the past several years started up again, and eleven counties in northern California sent a letter to their legislatures requesting the right to secede from the state."

"I've seen signs on Highway 5," Rick said, "and I've read about the current effort. They're very vocal about the fact that the ideas and laws coming out of Sacramento don't represent the beliefs of those who want to secede. Any idea on how their request now stands?"

"I don't, but I wouldn't discount their efforts. Those involved are pretty serious, and we may someday have a fifty-first state called Jefferson."

Rick laughed. "You're just full of little-known facts. How do you find time to learn all of this stuff?"

"I read a lot," said Patty. "And I'm glad you find it interesting. Now, changing the subject, want to share your thoughts about David Dorisko before we meet with him?"

Rick sat quietly for a minute. "We know that he has a key to the storage unit and, if we can believe his brother, the two of them have the only keys. He recently got out of prison. His brother said David had been involved with drugs but has been clean for the past few months. The fact that he has no residence suggests that his past has been a deterrent to his becoming educated or holding down a job. Could he be involved with the homicides? We can't rule him out at this time."

"So I'll ask the questions if you'll take notes," Patty said.

"For a change?"

"Well, you can jump in any time you think of something I haven't asked or want to lead him in a different direction."

Rick chuckled. "I got it."

The McDonald's wasn't hard to find, and pulling into the parking lot, the detectives saw a Eugene police car. Patty waved to the officer in the car. "It's always good when I call ahead and know that the local guys have our backs."

"It is," said Rick. "I just hope we never need them."

Gerold Dorisko's brother David was sitting in a booth when the detectives walked in.

"I'm actually a little surprised he's here," Patty said to Rick.

Rick agreed. "I'm more than a little surprised."

"Hello, Mr. Dorisko," Patty said as she and Rick sat down. "We appreciate that you're on time."

David looked a bit disheveled in his torn blue jeans and long-sleeved t-shirt. "Yep," he said, looking up at Patty.

"Can we buy you a Coke or coffee?" Rick asked.

"Sure," he said. "Coffee."

"Black?" Rick asked.

"No. Could you ask for three creams and five sugars?"

Rick nodded before leaving the table. Patty asked a few general questions before Rick returned with coffee for all of them. She then went over why they were there. "Have you spoken with your brother since we set up this appointment?"

"Yeah, but I don't know where that key is, and I don't know anything about those two dead people. So you're wasting your time talking to me."

Patty continued. "We just need to ask a few questions, and then we'll let you get on with your day."

David shrugged his shoulders and leaned back in his chair. "Go ahead," he said while brushing the long hair off his face and behind his ears.

"When did you move your stuff into your brother's storage unit?"

"I don't remember the exact date, but it was a few months ago."

"Would that have been before or after your stint in prison?"

David stared at his hands, folded together on top of the table. "Before."

"What kind of stuff did you store in the unit?"

"Old stuff I didn't use much anymore but that I didn't want to throw away. I just put it in some boxes and stuck them in with Gerold's stuff."

"And you haven't opened the unit since storing your stuff?"

"No."

Rick glanced at Patty and then leaned forward. "So you do have a key."

The young man looked up quickly. "No," he said.

"You just told us that you moved your stuff into your brother's unit and that you haven't opened the unit since then. So you do have a key."

The detectives watched as David looked up and to the right, a movement that some professionals think suggests lying or making up what is about to be said. "Well, I guess I did have one then, but I don't know where it is now."

Rick opened a file and slid a photo of the deceased woman over to Patty, and Patty slid it across the table, placing it in front of David.

"This is a photo of the woman found dead in your brother's storage unit. Did you know her?" Patty asked.

Patty and Rick both studied the face of the man sitting across from them. He winced and quickly looked up at Patty.

"I didn't know her," he said, pushing the photo back.

Rick pulled a second photo from the file and slid it directly in front of David.

"What about him?" Rick asked. "He's the other victim found in your brother's storage unit. The unit to which you have a key."

David looked at the photo of the second victim and then up at Patty as he slid the photo away. "Do you really expect me to recognize them? I don't know how they got into Gerold's storage unit. I didn't let anyone in."

Sitting back in his seat, the man drank more of his coffee. "If that's all you came out here for, I'd like to get on with my day."

Rick and Patty glanced at each other.

"We may have to go through your boxes in the storage unit," said Rick. "You don't have a problem with that, do you?"

The man, who until now had seemed docile during the interview, looked upset as he fidgeted in his seat, unfolded his arms and formed fists with his hands on top of the table. "Why would you want to go through my stuff? Am

I a suspect? I don't believe you can do that without a warrant. Why are you harassing me?"

"David," Patty said, "let me remind you that this is an investigation, and you have boxes stored in the unit where two people died, a unit for which you have one of only two keys. Did they go into your brother's unit to get something that someone else wanted? We need to know what is stored in your boxes."

Changing his attitude again, David sat quietly for a minute and then let out a sigh. He unclenched his fists, and his worried face relaxed to one of no expression. "Yeah, I understand. I'll be honest with you, Detectives. I haven't always been on the right side of the law, but I've paid my dues and I've been trying hard to live a clean and sober life. It's kind of frustrating to be suspected of any crime, especially when two people are dead. When do you want to go through the boxes?"

"When we get the warrant," Patty said as she stood up to leave. "We understand your frustration, and we appreciate your cooperation. We'll probably need to talk with you again, so before we leave, Rick needs to write down both your physical address and mailing address."

"I don't have a physical address," he said as he stood up to go. "I stay with friends and use general delivery at the post office for mail. So, how long does it take for you to get a warrant?"

Patty stood still and looked David in the eyes. "There's no set time, David. It could be three days or a week. Or it could be on my desk when I get back. Is there something in the boxes that you're concerned about?"

David breathed in heavily and exhaled quickly. "No," he said.

Rick nodded, and he and Patty followed David to the door. They watched him walk off down the block and then looked to where the Eugene police car still sat parked. The two detectives walked over to thank the officer and then got into their car.

Before Rick started the car, Patty asked, "Think he was lying?"

"He was lying," Rick said. "The condition of the victims makes them impossible to identify, but he knows more than he's giving us. He may know who killed them. We need to look at what's in those boxes."

"I agree," said Patty. "I'll ask Pete to check on the warrant." Patty made the call and gave Rick a thumbs-up.

On their return drive to Brookings, Patty's cell phone rang. "It's Doc Miller," she said, looking at caller ID. "Hi, Doc."

"Hey, Patty. Your victims died about a month ago. I'll be more exact after I've completed a couple of tests. In my opinion, they both died from their gunshot wounds. I found two 45-caliber bullets in her and a 9mm in him. I expect that ballistics may have no problem determining whether the 45 was shot from the 1911 found with the bodies. The 9mm, as you know, will be more difficult."

"Yeah, I know," said Patty. "The polygonal rifling inside the barrel on a Glock is hard to match to the bullet. There is no problem, however, matching a casing to the specific Glock. So if we can find the gun that was used, and it's a match with the casing, there is reason to believe that the bullet is from the same gun."

"Great deduction, Patty."

"Anything else you can tell us, Doc?"

"Only that there appears to be no other obvious trauma to the bodies. The tightly-closed storage unit kept rodents and animals away, and the moderate weather helped."

"Doc," asked Patty, "do you think it's possible the male victim shot himself?"

The ME paused a moment before speaking. "We'll do GSR testing on both bodies, but I expect there will be no gunshot residue. Furthermore, if he had shot himself, the wound channel would have been at a completely different angle, and the damage to the skull would have been much greater if he were shot at close range. So, to answer your question, no, I don't think he shot himself."

"Thanks, Doc. I'll relay all of this to the LT."

"And," said the ME, "you can tell your lieutenant that, in my opinion, you've got a double homicide."

CHAPTER FOUR

The lounge was intimate, with a seven-seat bar and five or six small tables. Vic Thompson worked behind the bar serving drinks. His medium build and close-cut hair made him an unassuming individual. He was, like many bartenders, skilled at listening to the stories of those who were frequent visitors. His personal story of once-upon-a-time heavy drug abuse was embedded into his face: lots of scarring from pustulosis and dark areas on the skin.

He kept the lights in the place dimmed to make the atmosphere romantic and the customers more attractive to each other. Over the Bose speakers Lou Rawls sang *Rainy Night in Georgia.* Vic's goal was to transport those who came through the front door into a world much different from the one they'd left outside. The encumbering effects of demanding bosses, unhappy spouses, or financial struggles were slowly replaced with the intoxicating mixture of drink, atmosphere, and a bartender who treated every patron like his best friend.

Vic noticed a change on the screen of the TV above one corner of the bar. A special news report had cut into the regular programming. While drawing a couple of draft beers he saw a Brookings police officer standing outside a storage unit talking to the newscaster. A few feet behind the officer stood a guy leaning against the unit. Vic finished the drinks and set them on a tray for the barmaid. He then stepped away from his customers and picked up the phone.

* * *

Suzie Mantis finished up her work for a real estate firm and drove home to be there by three o'clock when her nine-year-old daughter and eleven-year-old son arrived from school.

"Hi, Mom," the kids yelled when they came through the door and headed toward the kitchen.

"Hi, kids," Suzie said as she set their fruit and peanut butter snacks on the table.

"Is there something wrong?" asked her son.

"No. Why do you ask?"

"I don't know. You look like something's wrong."

Suzie laughed. "Everything's fine," she said. "I've just had a hard day."

The kids started on their snacks when the telephone rang, and Suzie picked up the wall phone in the kitchen. After listening briefly, her side of the conversation was clipped and direct. "I haven't had the TV on," she said. "What do you want to do? I don't think that's a good idea. Let me think about it and call you back." Suzie hung up the phone, cleaned up the dishes, and put the peanut butter away. She had a little more than two hours before her husband would be home.

"You know what, Mom?" said Heather. "We had birthday cake in class today for my friend."

"That's nice, honey. Are you finished with your snack?"

"Yeah, I'm done. Want to know what kind of cake we had?"

"I'm sorry, honey, but not now. I need for you and Billie to go upstairs and get started on your homework."

"Gosh, Mom," said Billie, "can't you first let her tell you about the cake?"

"No, I can't. Now please help me out and take your sister upstairs. I've got something I need to take care of."

Billie scowled. "Come on, Heather. Seems Mom's not in a very good mood."

Once the children were upstairs, Suzie picked up her cell phone and walked to her den, where she tapped in a phone number and heard the receiver pick up at the other end of the call.

"Yeah?"

"It's me," she said. "Vic just called. What's going on?"

"Nothing."

"Don't tell me nothing," Suzie demanded. "Vic saw the news. There was a murder in your brother's storage shed. What if they start investigating you?"

"The cops are not interested in me," said David. "They've got a murderer to catch."

"Well, I'm worried," said Suzie.

"Yeah? So maybe we should all meet."

* * *

It was nine in the morning and not too busy at Vic's. A couple in their forties sat at one of the tables drinking their breakfast while three men were at the bar nursing cocktails before leaving for another boring day at the office. Vic, Suzie, and David Dorisko sat at a corner table.

"So who're the homicide victims?" Vic asked David.

"I don't know yet. They haven't released the names."

"The cops are getting close," said Vic. "I told you we were going too far. You and your habit put us in this position."

Vic then turned his attention to Suzie. "And you should never have told that girl about us. You should have read her better."

"Look," Suzie said, "I told her because she was using and was interested in doing whatever was necessary to get out of her student debt. I didn't know she still had a conscience and a mother who would talk her into getting clean."

"So both of you shut up," said David. "We're going to be okay. The police have nothing on any of us."

"How do you know that?" asked Suzie.

"I know because they questioned me."

Vic sat back abruptly in his chair and then fell forward with both hands hitting the top of the table. "The police have questioned you?"

Suzie saw the three guys at the bar all look over at their table. "Keep your voice down, Vic. We don't need for someone here to call the cops."

Vic took his hands off the table and stared at David. "When did they question you?"

"Yesterday," David said. "But it's all cool. They don't have anything."

"That's easy for you to say," said Suzie. "You have nothing to live for other than your next hit. I have two kids and a husband who takes very good care of us."

"Hey," said David. "You should have thought of them before."

"I was thinking of them. I don't know why I let you talk me into this mess."

David smiled. "Sure you do. And our secret will remain a secret as long as we all just remain calm."

CHAPTER FIVE

Patty and Rick met with the sheriff's deputy and his canine at the storage unit. Rick had a camera hanging around his neck, and both he and Patty had nitrile gloves stuck in their pockets. Officer Bradley was also there at Patty's request.

Patty walked up to the deputy. "I'm Detective Patty O'Toole." She turned toward Rick and Brad to introduce each of them. "Detective Rick Starker and Officer Burt Bradley." Turning back to the deputy, she looked down at the dog. "That's a good-looking dog."

"Thanks," he said. "I'm Deputy Jake Browning and this is Bendix."

Patty smiled. "We appreciate you both helping us out. We received our warrant late yesterday, and we're eager to have Bendix look inside."

Rick knocked on the storage unit door. "Police. We have a search warrant." He opened the lock and rolled up the door.

Deputy Browning looked into the unit. "What do you suspect is in there?"

"We don't know that there's anything of interest," said Patty, "but one of two brothers with keys to this unit has drug history."

Jake looked around the room. "This will be easy. If there are drugs, Bendix will find them."

"That's what we're hoping for," said Patty. "What do you want us to do?"

"First I need to have the boxes that are stacked in the back rearranged so that the combined height isn't any higher than Bendix's neck when he stands on two legs. I usually require a precursory check for needles or anything else that can hurt the dog; however, I suspect that the sheets of heavy plastic on the floor are something you laid down to preserve the crime scene while we search."

Patty nodded. "The plastic was put down yesterday specifically for your dog, and no one's been in the unit since." She looked over at Brad. "Can you help us out here, Brad, and lower those back boxes?"

"Anything else?" Patty asked the deputy.

"You're good standing out here. Bendix needs to be able to move about freely. Considering this small a space, it shouldn't take long."

When Brad finished up, Jake unhooked the collar on Bendix and then spoke to the dog in a foreign language. Bendix immediately walked into the unit. He walked along one side to the back where he sniffed around several boxes. He then went to the opposite wall where his behavior changed.

"His tail is wagging like crazy," said Rick. "Does that mean he smells drugs?"

The deputy nodded. "It's one indicator. Another is his ears. See how they have perked up and back?"

The dog walked back and forth and then sat down facing one of the plastic buckets.

"Notice how the axis of his body has changed." said the deputy. "There are probably drugs in that bucket, but I need to make sure." He walked over to the dog and brought him back to the entrance of the storage unit, where he again let go of the leash. Bendix walked straight for the same plastic bucket. The deputy joined his dog and removed the lid from the container. "Looks like this bucket has been used for more than beer." He rewarded Bendix with a jute toy. "You probably want to use your gloved hands to remove the package."

Rick walked over, reached in and pulled out what appeared to be a plastic-wrapped kilo of cocaine. "Well, what do we have here? Looks like either our tenant is lying to us, or his brother's looking at more prison time."

Patty nodded and then turned back to Jake. "That was fast. It would have taken us several hours to open and go through every one of those boxes."

"Speed in finding the drugs," said Jake, "is one of the two great benefits of having a drug dog. The part of a dog's brain that is devoted to analyzing smells is, proportionately speaking, forty times greater than ours. They possess more than two hundred and twenty million olfactory receptors in their noses. Humans only have about five million."

"That's amazing," said Rick. "What's the other great benefit of using the dog?"

"We may catch a criminal without having to use our guns when we have an incident where the detained individual refuses to cooperate. The responsible may come away with a few nasty dog bites, but he or she won't get shot."

Patty reached out and gave Bendix a pat on the head. "How long did he train to become a drug dog?"

"Training for certification as a drug dog took one hundred and eighty hours. An equal amount of training was required for his certification as a bite dog. After being certified he's required to train for another sixteen hours each month."

Rick looked at the beautiful dog sitting calmly next to his handler. "Would he attack someone trying to injure you?"

"Absolutely, and that doesn't require a command."

Patty looked at the dog. "He's a great asset to the Sheriff's office." She then spoke again to Jake. "You mentioned beer. Is that type of bucket commonly used to make beer?"

"All of that equipment along the wall is used in beer-making. My brother-in-law makes beer and has all of the same stuff."

The detectives shook hands with Deputy Browning. "Thanks again for helping us out. It was great to see Bendix in action."

"Anytime, Detectives."

Patty glanced at the kilo and then at Rick. "Let's go back to the department, where we can have this checked into evidence. It'll be sent to the OSP state lab to be identified and processed for prints. Would you call Brad and ask him and Pete to pick up Gerold Dorisko and bring him in for possession? I'll let PO Lincoln know what we have so that she can pick up his brother, David. The warrant we have allows us to search for the remaining two casings. Let's meet back here with Brad and Pete after we interview Dorisko. The guys can move boxes for us."

* * *

Thirty minutes later, Gerold Dorisko sat in the interview room with Patty and Rick. "I know nothing about any drugs," he said.

Patty leaned back in her chair while Rick leaned forward.

"I'm sorry to hear that," Rick said, "because you're going to be charged with possession."

Gerold shook his head. "I'm telling you both, I didn't put the drugs there."

"Who do you think did?" asked Rick.

Gerold looked genuinely pained as he responded, "My brother."

Now Patty leaned forward. "You told us your brother's clean. That he's a nice guy. Why would he hide drugs in your storage unit, putting you at risk?"

Gerold sat up with a sudden movement as he responded to Patty. "That stuff doesn't belong to David, and I'll bet he didn't know what was in the plastic tub when he stored those things in my unit. You need to ask him about it."

"Do you know," Patty asked, "if any of your brother's friends make beer?"

"No," Gerold answered.

"Any of them sell drugs?"

Gerold stared down at the table. "He had several, but I never knew them. Dave said he'd quit hanging around with druggies. You'd have to ask him if he still sees any of them."

"We'll ask him," said Patty. "Right now, we're arresting you for possession of cocaine."

Gerold fell back in his chair. "Why?" he argued. "I'm telling you that it isn't mine."

Patty stood up. "It was found in your storage unit."

Rick stood up and told Gerold to put his hands behind his back, which he did without resistance.

"When will you talk with my brother?" he asked.

"Soon," said Patty as she walked to the door and opened it. Seeing Brad at the end of the hallway she called out, "Hey, Brad. Can you take Dorisko here to Gold Beach?"

Brad nodded. "Sure."

With Brad taking care of Dorisko, Patty and Rick returned to their desks, where Patty called Probation & Parole Deputy Lincoln. "Hello, Deputy. This is Detective O'Toole calling again about David Dorisko." Patty heard a sigh at the other end of the call.

"What's he done now?" she asked.

"We're not sure that he's done anything. But we've found what appears to be a sealed kilo of cocaine stashed in one of the items your offender stored in his brother's storage shed. Before sending it off to the state lab, we ran a test here in the department and it proved to be cocaine. We're going to have to question him again while we wait for lab results on fingerprints."

"I'll bring him in this afternoon," Lincoln said. "When do you want to meet with him?"

"Hold on and let me check with Starker." Patty put the call on hold and checked with Rick on his availability. Speaking into the phone again, she continued, "Starker and I can meet with Dorisko tomorrow afternoon at one. Can you set it up for us?"

"I can," said Lincoln.

"Thanks. We appreciate your help."

Rick looked up as Patty ended the call. "So, when do you want to leave here in the morning?"

"Eugene is about a four-and-a-half-hour drive. Let's make it 7:30 so that we don't have to worry about minor delays."

Officer Chekowsky knocked at the detectives' office door.

"Hey, Pete," Patty said. "What's up?"

Pete walked into the room. "Well, it may not be connected to your murder case, but a couple just called with a missing person's report. Said their daughter's missing."

"How long?" Patty asked.

"They're not sure, but it's been seven weeks since they've seen her."

"Seven weeks?" Rick asked. "Why are they only now reporting her missing?"

"The daughter attends College of the Redwoods and only comes home on some weekends or an occasional holiday. Her roommate called the parents here in Brookings asking if their daughter was home with them. She was concerned because she hadn't seen her for a while."

Patty looked at Rick who raised his eyebrows. "We should talk with them."

Pete gave Patty the couple's contact information. "I'll call PO Lincoln back and cancel tomorrow's appointment," Patty said to Rick. "Dorisko will be held for parole violation and will have no chance for bail if his prints are found on the kilo. We can interview him later in the week. I want to talk with this couple as soon as possible."

"It's kind of late today," Rick said. "You going to set up something for tomorrow morning?"

"How about nine?" Patty asked. Rick nodded. She looked at the note Pete had given her and tapped the Deboes' number into her phone.

"Is this Mr. Deboe?" Patty asked.

"Who's asking?"

"This is Detective O'Toole with the Police Department."

"Oh yes, Detective," he said. "Have you found our daughter?"

"I'm sorry, Mr. Deboe, but we need some additional information. Can you and Mrs. Deboe come to my office tomorrow morning?"

"We can do that," he said. "What time?"

"Nine o'clock," Patty said, "if that's not too early for you."

"It's not too early, Detective. We're not getting much sleep here."

Patty paused and then asked, "Will you please bring a current photo of your daughter and a personal item of hers such as a toothbrush or razor?"

Now it was Mr. Deboe who paused. "Our daughter is only missing, Deputy. Why would you need...?" Mr. Deboe's silence expressed great pain.

Patty spoke up, carefully choosing her words. "It's routine with missing persons cases, Mr. Deboe. We just want to be thorough."

"I see," he said. "We'll bring what you've asked."

"Thank you, sir. We'll see you tomorrow morning at nine."

Rick made note of the appointment and then closed the file on his desk. "I'm calling it a day," he said.

Patty glanced at her watch. "I should probably go home too. Let's meet at eight tomorrow morning at the storage unit to look for the remaining casings. I'll let Brad and Pete know we won't search today."

* * *

The next morning, Brad and Pete met the detectives at the storage unit as planned. It didn't take long before two additional casings were found. Patty gave them to Brad, signed the evidence log, and asked that he check them into the evidence room back at the PD.

Patty and Rick returned to the office in time for their nine o'clock meeting with the Deboes, who were waiting in one of the interview rooms. The distraught couple had bags under their eyes and red noses. Mr. Deboe sat hunched over as though he carried the weight of their worry on his back. Mrs. Deboe sat rigid, with her hands tightly clenched. It was clear that this was a very difficult time for them both. Rick offered coffee and brought cups in for the Deboes and himself.

Patty thanked them both for coming in and began the questioning. "What's your daughter's name?"

"June," said Mr. Deboe. "June Alice Deboe."

"And how old is she?"

He turned his head and looked at his wife as more tears escaped from her eyes. "She'll be nineteen next month."

"I understand," Patty said, "that she's attending the College of the Redwoods and lives with a roommate during the week. Is this correct?"

Mrs. Deboe spoke up. "She was coming home most weekends." There was a break in her voice, and she paused before continuing. The woman's hands were held together tightly, as though she didn't know what else to do with them. Her face expressed great pain as large tears broke free of her tired-looking eyes. "And sometimes during the week for a holiday." She slowly looked up at her husband. "At least she used to."

Rick continued to take notes while Patty proceeded with the questions. "Has she always told you when she wasn't going to be home on a weekend?"

The couple looked at each other, and Patty guessed they might be considering how much to tell the detectives.

"We need to understand," Patty said, "if we're going to be able to help."

"Not lately," said Mrs. Deboe.

Patty and Rick sat quietly waiting for the Deboes to continue.

Mr. Deboe broke the silence. "We think she got involved with the wrong kind of people. She seemed to become distant lately."

"The wrong kind of people?" Patty asked.

Mr. Deboe sighed. "She wouldn't tell us when we'd ask her what was wrong."

"I see," Patty said. "Did you bring the things I requested? A photo and a personal item?"

Mr. Deboe opened a bag he'd been holding, pulled out both a toothbrush and a razor, and laid them on the table. He then took out a framed photo and set it down next to the brush. Patty and Rick braced themselves as they looked at the photo. The young lady looking back at them had long blond hair and a beautiful smile.

"That's her high school photo," said Mrs. Deboe. "I'm afraid we don't have anything more current. Her roommate might have one."

Patty picked up the photo and looked at it. "Has she changed much since this photo was taken?"

Mrs. Deboe nodded her head. "She cut her hair short about six months ago and started dying it various colors. I think it was black the last time we saw her. Her roommate would know."

"Mr. and Mrs. Deboe," Patty began, "this is a difficult question to answer, but was your daughter June using drugs?"

The sad-looking couple glanced at each other again, and he put his hand over hers before answering the detective's question. "We've asked ourselves that very same question."

Mrs. Deboe dabbed her eyes with the tissue. "She was always such a good girl. Our only child. We suspected she might be using drugs because her personality changed. The last time she was home I spoke to her about the dangers of drugs. About what they do to the mind. I showed her diagrams I printed off the internet showing the effects of drugs on the brain. I told her we would help with her student debt. I hugged her and told her it would kill us to lose her. She assured me she wasn't doing drugs and that she'd just been depressed." Mrs. Deboe looked up sadly at Patty. "But something changed her during these past few months."

Patty paused a moment before asking, "Did she mention a boyfriend?"

Mr. Deboe breathed deeply. "She told us she had men friends, but nothing was serious."

"Thank you," Patty said. "We'll need the name and phone number of her roommate."

Mrs. Deboe took a piece of paper out of her pocket and handed it to Patty. "I figured you'd need it." She then turned her head and looked at Rick. "She's our only child. Please find her for us. It's cold out at night and she may not have her coat. We want her to come home. Please find her."

Rick looked at Patty and then spoke up. "We'll let you know as soon as we learn anything." He gave Mr. Deboe his and Patty's business cards. "You can call us anytime."

Mr. Deboe stood, helped his wife stand up, and put his arm around her. They slowly began to walk toward the door.

Rick quickly stepped in front of them and opened the door. As they walked out, Mr. Deboe turned his head and looked at Rick. "Thank you," he said.

As Rick saw the Deboes out the door, Patty picked up the photo and stared at it. "Are you our Jane Doe?" she quietly asked. She put the toothbrush and razor into evidence bags, signed and dated the log attached to each bag, and walked out of the room. She asked Pete to mail them to the lab in an overnight delivery box. "Send it to Doc Miller's attention. She'll get faster DNA results than we would and can match it up to what she has."

Patty returned to her office and found Rick already at his desk. "This job is just too hard at times," she said to Rick. "If we've got a match, how do we tell that man and his wife that their only child was murdered?"

Rick said nothing, knowing the question was rhetorical.

CHAPTER SIX

V ic Thompson was serving drinks to the after-work crowd when the phone
at the bar rang. After five rings he picked up.

"Hey, Vic," David greeted him.

Vic unintentionally quickly scanned the room for anyone who might be
paying too much attention. "What do you want?"

"That's not a very nice way to greet a friend."

Vic gritted his teeth and tightly grasped the phone. "You're not my friend,
and I told you not to call my bar phone."

"We've got a problem, Vic."

Vic turned his back to his patrons so that they couldn't see the maroon
color creeping up his neck. "What do you mean 'we'? What kind of a problem?" he demanded.

"Well, remember that kilo of cocaine we were saving for students like
Suzie's Miss June?"

"What about it?"

"Well, I kind of hid it in my brother's storage unit and the cops found it."

Vic paused to take in what this could mean for him. "How can you be so
stupid?"

"Hey, Vic. I didn't know at the time that there would be a double murder
in there."

"So tell the cops it belongs to your brother. It's his storage unit."

"Well, my friend, that might have worked if it wasn't my fingerprints they're going to find all over the plastic wrap around the coke."

Vic swore quietly into the phone, not wanting his customers to hear. "You're such a lowlife, Dorisko. I was stupid to have ever hung out with you. I've worked hard to get where I am, and I'm tired of your interference with my life. I don't know why I even answer your calls."

"Yes you do. It's all about our little secret. Just thought you'd want to know I'll be locked up for a while."

Vic hung up the phone and looked around. He wasn't rich, but over the past ten years he'd done alright for himself. He'd bought the lounge and developed a steady relationship with his girlfriend, who knew only that he was a successful businessman.

"Hey, bartender," someone called out. Vic picked up his bar towel, rubbed it over the top of his bar, and poured another malt liquor for his customer.

* * *

Suzie Mantis was having coffee with some of the other young mothers who had children in the same classes as Suzie's. They were talking about the latest in vacuum cleaners when one of the mothers said to Suzie, "You have the perfect life."

Suzie laughed. "Why do you say that?"

"Just look at your life. You have a fabulous house, a husband who adores you and not only doesn't mind but wants to take care of you and his kids. And your kids are both well behaved. What more could you ask for?"

Suzie smiled at her friend and thanked her. "I do feel blessed, but I don't think my life is really that much different from yours. And my life wasn't always like this." Her cell phone vibrated before she could go on.

"Suzie, it's Vic. Don't get mad at my calling you, just listen. David's locked up, and there's no chance of bail."

Suzie worked hard to keep her expression from showing the angst she now felt. "What happened?"

"The idiot hid his cocaine in his brother's storage unit and the cops found it. He figures his prints are all over it."

"I can't discuss this with you right now," she said, noticing that her friends had stopped talking and were watching her. "Let me call you back later."

"Sure. But there's nothing we can do. I just figured you'd want to know."

"Thanks," Suzie said before ending the call.

One of the women asked, "What's wrong, Suzie? You look a bit pale."

"I'm okay. Just a problem I'm working out with a neighbor."

* * *

Patty looked down at the name and phone number Mrs. Deboe had given her. "We need to talk with June's roommate, Sharon Stemen. Maybe she can lead us to people June hung around with. Okay for you if I try to set up an interview with her tomorrow? We'll probably have to meet her at the college campus in Eureka."

Rick glanced down at this calendar. "I'm expecting the LT to come down on me anytime now asking for my late reports. But, yes, I can go tomorrow."

Patty used her cell phone and input Stemen's number. The phone rang four times before going to voice mail.

"This is Sharon. You know the drill."

Patty waited for the beep and left a brief message asking for a call back as soon as possible. She closed the file and lifted her jacket off the back of the chair. "I'm calling it a day. I'll let you know if I hear from the roommate." Before Rick could respond, Patty's cell phone rang. "Detective O'Toole."

"Detective, this is Joe at the lab. We've got fingerprints off the plastic wrap around the kilo of cocaine you sent over. He's in the system and his name is David Dorisko."

"Son-of-a-gun," Patty said. "It is him."

"It's who?" asked Joe.

"A person of interest in a murder case."

"That the double murder in the storage unit?" Joe asked.

"The same," said Patty.

Joe continued with his questions. "Have you identified the victims?"

"Still waiting. There was no ID on either of them."

"Will Doc Miller be able to get fingerprints?"

"I don't expect so. The bodies were in a state of mummification."

"That makes it tough," said Joe.

"Yeah, but the doc says not to give up hope. The lab is working on it."

"Well, hope they come through with something for you."

"Thanks, Joe. And thanks for the call."

"Anytime, Detective," he said.

Patty gave the conversation details to Rick. "I'll call PO Lincoln, tell her about the prints, and let her know we can't get out there until later this week."

"Which means," said Rick, "that you can go home."

Patty took her purse out of the drawer. "Don't stay too late."

"I'm going to stick around and finish up one of these late reports. See you tomorrow."

CHAPTER SEVEN

Patty walked into her house and set her gun on the end table next to her favorite living-room chair. She then walked into the kitchen and opened the freezer door to peruse her choice of TV dinners. She chose a Marie Callender roasted turkey, placed it in the microwave, and tapped in three and a half minutes. Her cell phone rang while the microwave was turning the frozen concoction into a quick, tasty dinner. Caller ID showed it was her mother.

"Hi, Mom. I just got home. How's your day going?"

"Going great," Maggie said. "I just received my jury duty notice and can't wait to learn what case will be tried."

"That's great, Mom. I too will be interested in learning what case you get. When do you go in?"

"Next Wednesday. I hope they keep me on the jury even though I have a daughter who's a detective."

"I think there's a good chance they will, Mom. I heard that the wife of one of the sheriff's deputies was able to serve."

"Very reassuring," said Maggie. "So, are you and Rick working on anything interesting? Anything you can tell me about?"

"Not yet. But I'll keep you abreast of any new developments that I can talk about. Changing the subject, how is Bill doing?"

"He's doing great, Patty. He spent the day helping a neighbor who's building a greenhouse for his vegetables. Bill likes the physical work and the fact that it's keeping him busy."

"I'm happy to hear that," Patty said. "Do you two still walk every morning?"

"Most mornings."

"Have you started planning your next cruise?"

"Funny you should ask. Last night we decided on a vacation but not a cruise. This trip will be on both train and coach."

"What a great way to travel! What made you decide to travel by train?"

"I've never ridden in one," said Maggie. "Bill took the train to Reno a couple of times when he lived in California, but he's never spent the night on one. I've always wanted to find out if riding the train is as romantic as it's depicted to be in the old movies. We'll be on it two days and one night before transferring to a coach."

"What's your destination?" Patty asked.

"Let's see. We board the train in Chicago and travel west. We'll switch to a coach in Utah and then travel northeast to South Dakota. On the way we'll visit several national parks, a couple of dude ranches, and some famous old towns."

"Pretty exciting," Patty said. "I look forward to hearing about all the sights you'll see."

"And I look forward to telling you about them," said Maggie. "I'm especially interested in the South Dakota Black Hills area. You have a great aunt who taught school there and knew three Indian chiefs. Your cousin George was a cowboy and broke wild horses, among other things."

"I didn't know that, Mom. Seems you have family history you've not yet shared with me."

"I'll share more when we return from our trip."

"I'll need a copy of your itinerary, and the name and contact information for your tour company."

"I've already put it aside for you, dear. Well, I just wanted to check in with you. Say hi to Becky for me."

"I will. Give my best to Bill."

"Okay, dear. Love you."

"Good night, Mom. Love you too."

Patty pulled back on the plastic covering the dinner, moved the turkey and mashed potatoes around and hit the microwave button again. Three minutes later, she sat down to eat and Becky walked through the front door.

"Hi, Bec," Patty called out.

Without responding, Becky walked into the kitchen. Patty looked up to see her daughter crying. "Becky, what's wrong?" Patty asked as she quickly stood up and put her arms out.

"Oh, Mom," Becky cried as she dropped her book bag on the floor and stepped into her mother's open arms. "Josh is going to study abroad for a year. He leaves in September."

Patty gave her daughter a big hug. "It's not the end of the world, Bec, though I know it may feel like it. Where's he going?"

Becky released herself from her mom's hug and sat down at the table. "Ireland," she said. "He wants to study international business in Dublin, and because of his grades the university's offering him a one-year scholarship that includes room and board."

"Well, that's wonderful for Josh," said Patty. "Is this the first time the two of you have discussed this?"

"No. We talked about it when he submitted his application. I'm happy for him but the idea of him being gone a whole year didn't seem real until now. I'm going to be so very lonely."

"I'm sure that you'll get lonely at times, Bec, but there are many circumstances that separate couples during their marriage. If you are both thinking long-term with your relationship, you'll get through this."

Becky stood up and stared at her mother. "Why do you always have to be so darn practical? The man I want to spend my life with is going to leave me for a year. I don't care how many other couples spend time apart. I care about Josh and me, and I don't want us to be one of those couples."

"Let me ask you something," said Patty. "How often do the two of you see each other now?"

Becky thought about her mother's question. "I know where you're going with this, and it's different when we're living close to each other."

"How often?" Patty asked again.

"I guess about three times a month. And that's only because we're both carrying a full load. If we carried fewer credits, we'd see each other once or twice a week."

Patty laughed, and Becky responded by reaching for her bag.

"I'm glad you think this is funny, Mom."

"I'm sorry, Bec. But the reality is that you both do carry a full load and you only see each other a few times a month. Have you thought about what is really bothering you about his going to Ireland for a year?"

"I don't need to think about it."

"Becky, I disagree. So, as your mother, I'm asking you to give it some thought and let's talk again. Can we do that?"

"Okay. Right now I've got a paper to write."

Patty poured herself a glass of chardonnay and sat down to eat. She took a bite, shrugged, and ate her dinner cold. An hour later, she was in her favorite chair enjoying the wine when her cell phone rang. Patty recognized the caller ID area code as that of northern California. "Hello."

"Detective O'Toole?"

"Yes. Who's calling?"

"This is Sharon Stemen. June's roommate. You wanted to talk to me?"

"Thank you for calling back, Sharon. My partner Detective Starker and I would like to ask you a few questions about June. Would you be available tomorrow morning at nine? We can meet you at the Eureka college campus if you like."

"Nine will be fine, but I'd rather meet you at the coffee shop on Fifth Street downtown."

Patty agreed and called Rick to let him know they'd need to leave early.

* * *

The following morning Patty walked into the office to find Rick working on a report. "It's about seven," she said. "Ready to go?"

Rick set the file in a desk drawer. "Sure," he said as he stood and felt for his gun with the inside of his right arm.

"Was feeling for your gun something you learned in the academy?" Patty asked.

Rick nodded. "That's when I made it a habit."

"Were you trained to do that? I ask because I wasn't. So I'm wondering if it was something unique to your instructor."

Rick looked at Patty and then down at the floor. He ran his fingers through his hair.

Patty laughed. "What is it? I thought I asked a simple question."

"Yeah, well," Rick said. "It's pretty embarrassing."

"How can checking for your gun be embarrassing? You have now piqued my interest, so you have to explain."

"I showed up at the academy one morning with my holster on but no gun in it."

Patty smiled. "That's not good."

"No, it wasn't," Rick said, "and to make sure it didn't happen again, I had to walk around with a banana in my holster for two days."

"No!" Patty said, struggling not to laugh again.

Rick shook his head.

"Okay," Patty said, "I get it. After that you made it a habit to feel for your gun and make sure it's there. Has it worked?"

"I've not forgotten it since. So can we hit the road now?"

"You can drive," Patty said.

After driving through Crescent City Rick drove Highway 101 into the redwood forest.

"I never get tired of this stretch of highway, where I'm reminded of the beautiful area we live in."

"This is a scenic stretch of road," Patty said. "Too bad it's also such a dangerous area. Millions are spent every year on repairs to Last Chance Grade, and I've read where the cost of possible solutions ranges from three hundred million to a billion dollars. Like Oregon's Hooskanaden area, the three miles of Last Chance Grade roadway are moving all the time."

"I don't recall reading of any recent accidents along here," said Rick, "so they must do a pretty good job of maintaining the road."

Rick turned a corner, and a giant statue of Paul Bunyan and his blue ox stood across the street in front of the nature attraction called "Trees of Mystery." "How old did you tell me this park is?" he asked.

"Built in 1946," said Patty. "There are several trails that visitors can walk, and one is dedicated to the mythology of Paul Bunyan. When I went through as a kid there was no shuttle. Now you can board a shuttle and ride through the treetops."

"So, Miss History," said Rick, "what can you tell me about Eureka?"

Patty smiled. "Eureka means 'I have found it,' which is the official motto of the state of California. Eureka is the only city to use the same seal as the state."

An hour later, Rick pulled into the parking lot of the Fifth Street coffee house. "How do you want to handle this?"

"I suspect she'll have information that will be valuable in learning why June is missing. Why don't I start the questioning and you jump in anytime?"

"That works for me. But there's a chance we won't get anywhere with her if she's involved with the same people and their drug business. We may need to convince her that if they're responsible for June missing, these people may come after her too."

CHAPTER EIGHT

The young woman was sitting alone at a window booth. Patty approached and asked, "Are you Sharon Stemen?"

"Yes," she said. "Are you any closer to finding June?"

"No," said Patty as she sat down. "We're hoping you can help us."

The young girl shrugged her shoulders. "Sure, if I can."

After the introductions, Rick stood up. "Would you like a coffee, Sharon?"

"Sure," she said. "I'll have a decaf non-fat vanilla latte with whipped cream."

Rick looked at Patty and she noticed his deer-in-the-headlights look. "Why don't I get the coffee?" she offered.

Five minutes later, Patty set the warm mugs on the table. She took a sip from hers and then looked up at Sharon. "How long have you known June?"

"Two years. We met in our freshman year."

"Have you been roommates the whole two years?"

"No. We had different roommates the first six months or so of our freshman year. June's roommate transferred to another school and I took her place."

"Have you met June's parents, Mr. and Mrs. Deboe?"

"Once when June invited me to her house over a three-day holiday. How are they doing?"

Rick and Patty both watched the expression on Sharon's face. Patty responded, "They're scared."

Sharon nodded her head. "I'm not surprised."

Patty sat back in her chair and let Rick take over.

"Has June been using drugs?" he asked.

Both detectives could read in Sharon's face her reluctance to answer Rick's question as her eyes looked up and to the right.

"We can't have you making up answers," Patty said. "We need the truth from you."

"Sharon," Rick said, "we don't know if June is still alive. She could be lying hurt someplace or be with people who plan to hurt her. The sooner we find her, the greater her chance of survival. So please answer our question. Has June been using drugs?"

Sharon nodded her head. "Yeah. For about six months."

"And you?"

"No. My parents are paying for my education and would definitely turn off the funding if I started playing around with drugs."

"You use the term 'playing around,'" Patty said. "Is that what June's been doing?"

"Yeah. She was approached by some woman on campus who promised June she'd make enough in a few months to pay off her tuition loans. Said all she had to do was sell a few drugs to the other students."

"So she's been selling too?" asked Rick.

"Just for the past few months. She felt uncomfortable about it at first. But then when she saw the money she could make and took some of the stuff herself, she didn't care enough to stop. At least not until about seven weeks ago, when there seemed to be a change."

"A change?" Patty asked. "Tell us about that. Why do you think she changed?"

"Well, I'm not sure I can explain it. She went home for a day to see her parents, and when she came back, she told me she was going to stop using and selling the drugs."

"Did she say anything to you about why she wanted to stop?" Patty asked.

"Not specifically, but I got the impression that her parents must have spoken to her. She did say that she realized how stupid she was to have gotten mixed up with the whole thing and that she was going to tell the woman who introduced her to the drug scene that she no longer wanted to be a part of her group."

Rick and Patty glanced at each other.

"Do you know if June did tell the woman she wanted out?" Patty asked.

"She did."

"When?" asked Rick.

"I don't know. I guess right after she told me she was going to quit."

"Sharon," Patty said, "this is very important. Try to remember the day June told you she'd spoken with the woman."

Sharon pulled out her cell phone and looked at the calendar. "It was five weeks ago. The day of our government class exam."

"Did you ever see this woman?" Patty asked.

"No. Like I said before, I want nothing to do with the drug scene."

"Okay," said Patty. "That's all the questions I have." Patty looked at Rick.

"Just one more question," he said. "Do you have a current photo of June?"

"I probably have a couple on my phone. Give me your email address and I'll send them to you."

Patty and Rick gave their business cards to Sharon. "Call us," Patty said, "if you think of anything else."

The detectives left and started the drive north to Brookings.

CHAPTER NINE

The following morning Rick and Patty were at their desks when Patty's cell phone rang. She glanced at caller ID before answering.

"Hey, Doc. Got an ID on our female victim?"

"Nothing yet, Patty. But the lab tells me they're working on something that should help. They're trying a technique that is not well-known."

"That's great, Doc. We suspect that our female could be a missing college student, but we're reluctant to tell her parents without a positive ID. We'll have to let them know soon. Anything else you can tell us?"

"Not now. I just wanted you to know that the lab should have something for you soon."

"Thanks, Doc."

"You and Rick be safe out there."

"We will."

Patty gave Rick the details of the conversation. "I need to let the LT know what's going on. You want to run through what we've got before I tell him?"

Rick pulled his lined yellow pad from a drawer. "Let's start with two unknown victims, including a man who was shot once in the head by someone using a Glock. He was found holding a 1911 in his hand, a position meant to make it look like a suicide. The second victim is a young female shot twice with a .45 that we expect to be the 1911 found at the scene."

Patty tapped a pencil on her desk. "The storage unit in which the bodies were found belongs to a Gerold Dorisko, and Gerold's brother David holds the duplicate key."

"And the kilo of coke," Rick said. "We know it was David's."

Patty underlined one of her notes. "And then we have a missing college student, June Deboe, who could be our female fatality. June had been taking and selling drugs up until shortly before she died. According to her roommate, she ceased both activities five to six weeks ago.

"The roommate also said that within that same time frame, June spoke with the woman she bought drugs from on campus and said she wanted out. This may show cause for her death if our deceased is June Deboe."

Rick looked up at Patty. "So where do we go from here?"

Patty nodded her head as she thought. "We need for the lab to find something that identifies our Jane Doe. Let's continue working on the June Deboe case, knowing that there is a good likelihood that June is our deceased female. We need to talk with her teachers and the students she hung out with."

Rick nodded. "Identifying our male may have to wait. I'd like to interview David again now that we know he was dealing. And what about Gerold? Do you think he's as innocent as he wants us to believe?"

"I don't know, but we do need more information on David's past, and Gerold might be the one to give it to us. Why don't you try getting Gerold in here this afternoon? I'm going to call the college admissions office, find out who June's teachers were, and set up appointments. These appointments may take a couple of days. Work for you?"

"It does," said Rick. "We need to keep things moving as quickly as possible."

Patty stood up. "I'll update the LT while you arrange our meeting with Gerold Dorisko."

The venetian blinds on the lieutenant's office windows were open, making it possible for him to see Patty before she knocked.

"Come in, O'Toole," he said, using only her last name, which was his manner.

"Hi, LT. Got time for an update on the double homicide?"

He pointed to a chair as an invitation for Patty to sit down. "I do."

Patty filled the lieutenant in on both the murders and the missing persons case.

"How do you plan to proceed?" asked the lieutenant.

Patty explained what she and Rick had planned for the next couple of days.

"That sounds reasonable," he said. "There are often more people associated with a homicide than those found at the scene. And it's been my experience that if you can find the others, one of them will talk. The involvement of drugs could make your investigation a little easier. The world of drug users and dealers tends to attract people with no regard for trust or loyalty. They'll tell everything they know to decrease a personal jail sentence or prison term. They can also be desperate, which can make them very dangerous. You and Rick be careful."

"We will, LT. Thanks."

* * *

Suzie was drinking her second cup of coffee after the kids had gone to school. She sent a text to Vic, hoping this would all go away soon. *Got time to talk?*

Three minutes later he texted back to her. *Yeah. This is good. My barmaid's just arrived. Call now.* Suzie tapped his number into her phone.

"Hello," Vic answered.

"Vic, it's Suzie. This is the first chance I've had to return your call. I'm getting more and more worried, and I don't like knowing the cops are talking with David. Why would they think he had anything to do with those murders?"

"There's nothing yet that suggests the cops think that," said Vic. "The only reason they're watching him so carefully now is the cocaine. The cops won't be able to connect us with that coke."

"Not unless David talks," Suzie said coldly.

"He won't. Look, it was stupid for him to hide the stuff in his brother's locker, but like he said to me, how was he to know it would be the site of a double homicide? You need to remain calm, Suz."

"Oh no."

"What's wrong?"

"Gotta go. My husband just drove into the driveway."

* * *

Patty's desk phone rang, and she noted the call was from their department receptionist. "Thanks," she said before hanging up. She looked at Rick, who was working on one of his reports. "That was the front desk. Pete has Gerold in the interview room."

Rick closed his file and followed Patty down the hall. Gerold was seated with his back against the wall so that he could be watched through the one-way window. Before the detectives could sit down, he spoke.

"I've told you all I know. Is there something you need to ask that you couldn't ask me over the phone?"

Rick sat back with his lined pad and a pen. Patty sat forward.

"Gerold," she said. "You have a problem. You rent a storage unit in which there's been two murders and in which we have found a kilo of cocaine. You told us that your brother had been reformed. That he'd stopped using drugs. But his fingerprints are all over the drug package we found in your unit. So I guess he's not the man you thought he was."

"Or," said Rick, "you've been lying to us."

The room went silent and the detectives waited for Gerold to speak. A small bead of sweat made its way across his forehead, and a light shade of red lit up his cheeks and nose. "I didn't lie to you," he said. "I just told you what David told me. I know now that he was lying to me."

The detectives ignored Gerold's statement.

"Tell us about your brother's friends," said Rick.

"I told you before. I really didn't know them. It's not my scene."

"You may not have known them well," said Rick, "but you must have met some of them. Maybe at a party or at your brother's house?"

Gerold fidgeted in his chair as he spoke. "He used to hang out with some guy who made beer."

Rick and Patty glanced at each other. Rick asked, "Do you think it's his equipment that's in your storage unit?"

"I don't know."

"But you've met this guy," Patty said. "What does he look like?"

"I only met him a couple of times, and the only thing I remember is that he looked hard, like the pictures you see of long-time drug users. I remember thinking that I didn't want David ending up like that."

"How tall is he?" asked Patty.

Gerold rubbed his hand on his thighs as though trying to rub the sweat off his palms.

"He was medium build."

"How do you know he made beer?" Patty asked.

"David invited me to a party a couple years ago at the house he was renting. Some of them were drinking beer, and this guy was talking about his brewing process."

"Where was the house?" Patty asked.

"I don't remember. I was only there once."

Rick looked up from his notes. "Did you use the GPS in your car to get there?"

"I don't have GPS. I looked at a map. And it doesn't make any difference. David only lived there a couple of months."

Patty continued with the questioning. "Besides beer, what do you remember about the conversations at the party?"

"Come on," Gerold said, throwing his head back. "That was two years ago."

"So think hard," Patty said. "You drove to Eugene so you must have stayed a few hours to make the trip worthwhile. Maybe even stayed the night at your brother's place. Think for a minute and tell us what else you remember."

Gerold looked around the room as though he'd somehow find an answer within the four walls. "I don't know. I guess they talked about girls, drugs, and beer."

"Was their talk all about what they were using, or did anyone talk about dealing?"

"It was just their personal stuff," said Gerold. "Well." He looked down at his hands, now folded together on top of the table, and paused as though remembering something.

"Well?" Patty asked.

"There were a few women, and I remember that one mentioned something about selling."

"What was her name?"

"I don't know."

"What did she look like?"

"I didn't pay much attention to her. She was older than the other women. I remember thinking she was kind of out of place. She had a wedding ring on, but I couldn't tell that any of the guys were with her."

"What did she say that made you think that she might be dealing?"

Gerold looked at Patty. "She seemed sort of business-like. You know. I don't think she was enjoying the party, and I remember that she wasn't sampling the drugs."

"Not sampling the drugs," said Patty, "doesn't make her a dealer. So she must have said something that made you think she was."

Gerold paused again. "She never used the word 'dealing,' but I remember she said she'd had success on campus. She mentioned the lost souls who were so easy to persuade. She called them a bunch of immature kids who were so lonely that they'd do anything to have her befriend them."

"Was she talking about the University of Oregon?"

"I didn't hear her say the name of a school. I guess it could have been U of O."

"Anything else you remember about the woman or conversations?" asked Patty.

"No. The woman wasn't there long, and I only stayed a couple of hours."

Patty looked at Rick, who then directed the next couple of questions to Gerold. "Have you seen her again?"

"No."

"What about the guy who makes beer? Have you seen him again?"

"Just once when he helped David move his stuff into my storage unit."

"How do we find this guy?"

"I don't know. He kept to himself when they were moving the stuff. Maybe David knows."

"Is there anyone else besides the guy who makes beer that you've seen again since that party?"

Gerold slowly moved his head left then right. "No. And I never went to another one of David's parties. Most of the people there looked pretty messed up."

The detectives completed the interview and walked back to their office. Patty looked at her phone calendar for the following day. "Our first interview at the college is on Monday at nine, so we should leave Brookings about six forty-five."

Rick nodded. "No problem. I'd like to take off early today and take care of some personal business. Okay with you?"

"Sure. Go and enjoy your weekend," said Patty.

"You too," said Rick.

CHAPTER TEN

Rick and Patty got an early start back to the Eureka college for three interviews scheduled with June Deboe's teachers.

Rick was driving while Patty talked about the case. "It's looking like the guy Gerold met who makes beer may also own the beer equipment in the storage unit."

"Yeah," said Rick. "We need to talk with him. Find out if he knows one or both of the deceased."

"There's something else, Rick. Gerold said the woman at the party bragged on selling to students on campus. Think there's a possibility that she's the same woman Sharon mentioned, who sold to June?"

"I hadn't thought of that," Rick said. "Eureka is a long way from Eugene, but it's possible."

The detectives rode in silence for a while before Patty asked, "How'd your weekend go?"

"It was okay. Barbara and I had dinner together. She says she has a handle on her time now and wants us to try again."

"How do you feel about that?" asked Patty.

"I'm open to giving it another chance."

A few more minutes passed before Patty spoke again. "We have a mandatory qualification coming up, so I think I'll go to the range tomorrow. Are you ready?"

"Yeah, I'm good."

Rick drove through Klamath and had just crossed the Klamath River bridge when the detectives saw a CHP officer parked up ahead with his lights flashing. At first glance, it appeared as though he'd pulled over an RV for a traffic violation. As they drove closer, they saw a woman standing next to the officer and a man with a toddler in his arms standing next to the RV about thirty feet away. Rick lit up the car and pulled in behind the officer. He and Patty could now hear the woman's screams. The man held the toddler under one arm and a knife in the opposite hand. The officer periodically pulled the woman back when she'd begin to move toward the man.

"Call dispatch," Patty said to Rick, "and let them know where we are. I'll talk with the officer."

Patty approached the officer, showed her badge, and asked loudly, "Need help?"

"Yeah. Can you direct traffic around us? I've got backup on the way."

"We'll do that."

Patty let Rick know what they'd been asked to do. The detectives quickly removed the orange cones kept in their trunk and blocked off the lane closest to the incident. Rick then stopped traffic going north while Patty stopped it going south. The sirens of additional help could be heard in the distance, and within a couple of minutes, four Del Norte County Sheriff's deputies and several additional CHP officers were on the scene. When two of the deputies took over for the detectives, Patty and Rick walked back to the scene where the screaming continued. One of the CHP officers was now attempting to get the man to drop the knife.

"Don't hurt my baby," the woman screamed. "Don't hurt my baby."

The CHP officer was calling the man by his name. "Thomas, my name is Officer Welby."

"Stay away from me," the man yelled. "Stay away or I'll hurt the baby."

The officer took another step forward. "Why are you doing this, Thomas? What do you want?"

"I just want to leave in my RV and be left alone. I want to take my son with me."

"I can't allow you to take the baby with you, Thomas. Not when you're threatening to hurt him. Why don't you put down the knife?"

Patty watched as two of the CHP officers walked around the back of the trailer and positioned themselves about fifteen feet behind the man.

The officer talking with Thomas now took another step forward.

This caused the man to yell and wield his knife around. "Don't come any closer or I'll use this. If I can't keep my son, she won't have him either."

"Don't let him hurt my baby," the woman screamed.

Rick looked at Patty and saw tears flowing down her cheeks. "Do you want to go back to the car?" he asked her.

When Patty didn't answer, he asked again. "Patty, are you okay? Do you want to leave now?"

Patty looked at Rick, brought her hands up to her face, and wiped the tears away. "I can't," she said. "I want to know that the baby is safe."

Rick nodded and continued to stand next to her as the incident continued.

The officer yelled out again. "This is not going to work out well for you, Thomas. You said you want to leave and be left alone. We can't let you leave while you're holding both a knife and the baby. Drop the knife."

"Okay," he said. "If I drop the knife, will you let me leave with my son?"

"No," screamed the baby's mother.

The officer holding the mother back asked Rick to hold onto her. With his hand on his gun he slowly walked forward, providing backup for Welby.

"Drop the knife, Thomas, and you can leave with your son."

Thomas slowly lowered his arm and dropped the knife. The two officers behind Thomas quickly ran forward. One grabbed the toddler while the other took Thomas to the ground. The officer who'd been doing the talking ran up to help subdue the man and put him in cuffs. He then took hold of the toddler and carried him back to his sobbing mother.

Rick looked at Patty, who seemed to have composed herself. She wiped the tears from her cheeks and looked at Rick. "We should get going."

They had turned to walk back to their car when the officer first on the scene interrupted them. "Thanks for your help. We'll take the woman and baby back to the department. DHS will care for the child until we've confirmed the woman is his mother."

"You're welcome," Rick said. "Glad it ended the way it did."

Rick started up the car and pulled out onto the highway.

"Let's go back to Brookings," Patty said.

"You don't want to try and reschedule the appointments on our way to Eureka?"

"No. I want to go back to the department. Turn around."

"I'll turn around next chance I get. Are you okay?"

Rick could see the tears flowing again down Patty's cheeks, and she now began to shake. Her tears turned into sobs as she rested her head in the palms of her hands.

Rick lit up the car and turned it around. "We're on our way back, Patty."

A few minutes later she stopped crying. "I'm sorry, Rick. I don't know why that happened. You can turn off the lights."

Rick entered Brookings, pulled into the department parking lot, and they walked to their office. Patty went straight to her desk while Rick stopped in the kitchen to get coffee for each of them. He set her cup down on the side of her desk. "We need to talk, Patty."

"No, we don't. I'm okay."

"Well, I'm glad you're okay," Rick said, "but I'm not. I want to know what happened back there."

"Nothing I want to discuss."

"Look," he said, "I'm your partner and I do want to discuss it. Are you sick?"

"No, I'm not."

"Then you need to tell me what happened. And if you don't want to talk with me, you need to see the department psychologist."

Tears began to form in Patty's eyes as she looked at Rick and sat quietly.

He put his hand on her shoulder. "We can't just forget it, Patty."

Patty stood up and walked over to the door to their office. She closed it and walked to the window, where she stood staring outside, lost in her thoughts. "That's the first time I've experienced any fallout on the job. It surprised me as much as it surprised you."

"Fallout from what?" Rick asked as he walked up to join Patty at the window.

Patty slowly turned to face him. "A shooting."

"Shooting? When? Who?"

"It happened about two years into the job. I was on my way up to a search-and-rescue class in Gold Beach when a call came over the radio that a break-in was in progress at the Whaleshead development. That was during a time when the Sheriff's Office had only a handful of deputies and they were scattered across the county. State police reported that the nearest OSP officer was almost an hour away in Port Orford. So I responded and asked for backup. I could hear the woman's screams from inside the cabin as I drove up. Some of the other residents were already gathering on their porches."

Tears were streaming down Patty's cheeks as she seemed to be reliving the incident.

"Do you need to stop?" Rick asked. "Take a drink of coffee?" Rick wasn't sure she could hear him as Patty continued.

"The front door of the cabin opened, and a woman walked out. 'She's got my baby,' she screamed. 'Don't let her hurt my baby!' A second woman then appeared at the door with her left arm wrapped around a baby and a large knife in her right hand.

"'This is my baby,' the woman with the knife yelled. 'I'm not leaving without her.' She then pointed the knife toward the baby's mother and screamed, 'Tell her to stay away or I'll use this.'

"'I hear what you're saying,' I yelled out. 'I understand what you want. You don't have to do this.'

"I then asked the mother to walk over to me, which she did. I asked her to stay next to my car while I got her baby back. I stepped toward the woman on the porch. 'My name's Detective O'Toole. What's your name?'

"'Stay where you are,' she yelled. 'Don't come any closer.'

"'I'm right here, ma'am,' I told her. 'I'd just like to talk with you a minute.

Do you have other children?'" Patty paused, remembering the scene, then she continued explaining to Rick. "The woman with the knife seemed to slump a bit and become a little confused so I took a chance and asked, 'What happened to your other baby?'

"'The other baby?' she asked me. Then she looked around and saw the residents watching. She looked at the baby in her left arm and then up at me, and she started to cry. 'The baby died.'

"'I'm so sorry,' I said. 'What a tragic, tragic thing to happen. I'm sure you loved that baby.' The woman, tears falling off her cheeks, nodded.

"I took two more steps forward. 'I know that you don't want this baby to die too, do you?'

"'No,' she cried.

"I was then only about five feet away from the woman. I started walking up to her with my arms out. 'You're a good mother,' I said to her. 'Give me the baby.'

"The woman loosened her grip as I gently took the baby from her arms. But when I started backing up, the baby's mother left the side of my car and ran toward me with her arms outstretched. 'No,' I yelled, but it was all happening too fast. The woman with the knife raised it, screaming, 'You can't have my baby,' and lunged toward the baby's mother, wielding the knife. I drew my weapon and yelled at her to stop, but she caught up with the mother in just a few steps, bringing the knife down over the mother's outstretched arm. The baby's mother screamed as the other woman raised the knife again. That's when I fired."

Rick put his arm around Patty, walked her over to her desk, and helped her to sit down.

"I'll get you some water," he said.

"Wait, Rick. Let me finish. The incident today. It was like fourteen years ago all over again. The baby being held hostage by someone wielding a knife. The mother screaming not to let her baby get hurt. It took me back to the fear and sadness of it all. And in my mind, I could see the woman I shot falling to the ground."

"Patty. I'm assuming you were cleared, given the circumstances."

Patty nodded. "The baby's mother was badly cut. There were plenty of witnesses, resulting in no question about my having taken the right action. I went through the required counselling before returning to work and believed I had put it behind me. Today was the first time in all these years that I've reacted as I did this morning."

"Let me get you a glass of water," Rick said.

He returned with the water and sat silently, waiting for Patty to talk.

"How can something like this morning happen? How can my mind react to something that happened so long ago?"

"It's a form of PTSD. I experience it periodically, due to the sudden loss of Claire and Skylar. What happened to you was traumatic for your mind, and a healthy mind does not erase our experiences. It simply stores them. I know you, Patty. You must have suffered greatly due to having taken the life of that young woman. The fact that it was justified doesn't erase your humanity. What happened this morning may never happen again, but if it does, you'll probably handle it better next time because you'll recognize what it is."

Patty pulled a few tissues from her drawer, wiped her face, and blew her nose. "I'm sorry I didn't tell you sooner. There have been several times when I was going to, but it just didn't make sense to bring it up."

"No need to apologize. I think I understand. But now that you've told me, I need to ask if you think you should see a counselor again."

"No," said Patty. "Like I said, this was the first time anything like this has happened. Talking about it to you makes me feel like a weight's been lifted from my chest. Thank you for listening."

"You've done the same for me. I'm glad I was with you."

Patty looked into Rick's eyes. "I am too."

Seconds passed and neither of them spoke as Rick placed his hand over Patty's. Patty's eyes watered and a tear broke loose. She looked at their hands.

"I think I'd better go home," she said. "Get some rest. You should too."

Rick breathed in deeply. "I've got a report to finish," he said. He looked up to see his partner walk out the door.

* * *

Rick started on his report but found he couldn't concentrate, so he put away his files and left for home. Patty's experience had shaken him. He was reminded of the many times after Clare and Skylar's murders when a wave of deep grief had hit him out of the blue, causing him to pause in whatever he was doing. He was reminded of the many nights he'd left work dreading the lonely evenings that were in front of him and knowing he'd drink away the pain, at least for one more night. Standing next to Patty today, hearing the fear and pain coming through the words she'd spoken while reliving her experience made him want more than anything to put his arms around her and hold her close. But he couldn't, and knowing that made him want a drink. It had been three years since Patty had confronted him with his drinking, and every day for three years he'd reminded himself why he needed to remain sober. He turned off the main road home and headed for the location of the evening's AA meeting. He told himself that if he could live through the loss of his wife and daughter, he could get through another day without a drink.

CHAPTER ELEVEN

A few blocks from home, Patty's hands-free car phone system alerted her that she had a call from her mother.

"Detective O'Toole," she answered, knowing that's what her mother wanted to hear.

"Hello, dear, it's your mother. How's your day gone?"

"Hi, Mom. It's been a long day. How's yours been?"

"Patty, have you been crying?"

"Why would you think that?"

"Because your voice changes after you've been crying. It becomes a bit raspy and I can tell the difference. So tell me what's wrong. What has made you cry?"

"You're amazing, Mom. Do you know that?"

"Well, yes, dear, I do. At least sometimes. Well, maybe only now and then. Now tell me: what's made you cry?"

"I'm almost home. Can I call you back in five minutes?"

"Of course. I'll wait by the phone for your call."

Patty pulled into the driveway of the house she'd bought for herself and her daughter Becky, following the divorce from Becky's father. The small three-bedroom, two-bath home had become Patty's haven. She walked in, took out her gun and laid it on the end table as was her habit before doing anything else. She filled a tall glass with ice water, took off her shoes, got comfortable in her favorite chair, and called her mother back.

"I told Rick today about the Whaleshead incident. I told him everything."

"Was there something that triggered your telling him?"

"There was, Mom. This morning Rick and I came upon an incident off the highway. CHP was already there. A man was holding a toddler under his arm and a knife in the other hand, threatening to hurt the child. The toddler's mother was there screaming at him not to hurt her baby. I didn't mean for it to affect me the way it did, but I guess the circumstances were close enough to the incident at Whaleshead that my mind went back there, and I reacted."

"What do you mean you reacted, Patty?"

"Exactly that, Mom. I was right there hearing and seeing the crisis unfold. It was just so frightening and sad. I started crying."

"I'm sure it was difficult, dear, and I'm sorry you've had to revisit your own traumatic experience. It doesn't surprise me that, even this many years later, you would have a reaction to a similar incident."

"It was so unexpected, Mom. That scares me as much as the fact that I broke down. I don't want this to happen again. How can I continue to work?"

"Patty? Did you also tell Rick about the numerous letters you wrote for years after the event, imploring our state congressmen and senators to provide more and better mental health care services in Oregon? Do you remember writing those letters?"

"Sure I remember, Mom. But the only thing that evolved out of that effort was a lesson in futility for me."

"I know that's what you think, Patty, but that's not true. First, you planted a seed in the minds of those politicians, and you don't know if any of them might be willing to pick up the ball now and run with it. Secondly, and in my mind just as importantly, is what writing those letters did for you. You had learned that the family of the knife-wielding woman had tried for years to get help for her and had been denied because she hadn't caused anyone else any bodily harm. They knew that she was unstable, yet their pleas were ignored. Your efforts were made on behalf of all people who have family members in need of mental health and who have been unable to access the necessary services. Helping others helped you to heal, Patty. And I'm thinking this might be a good time for you to begin writing letters again."

"You've given me a lot to think about, Mom."

"Well, I'm glad you're going to give it some thought. You might want to talk with Rick about your effort. He may want to work with you."

"I never thought of involving Rick. I'll talk with him."

"Good," said Maggie. "And one more thing. Your job puts you into positions of having to make decisions that millions of people will never have to make, and you must make those decisions in seconds. You're a good person, Patty O'Toole, and a great detective. You made the right decision fourteen years ago and you'll continue to make good decisions. Now, sleep well tonight so that you and Rick can catch the bad guys tomorrow."

Patty couldn't help but laugh. "I will, Mom. Thanks."

"I love you too, dear."

* * *

The day began like any other for Suzie Mantis. She saw the kids off to school, put a load of laundry in the wash, and scheduled lunch with her friends for the following day. About eleven-thirty her cell phone rang. It was her husband.

"Hi, hon," she answered.

"Hi, Suzie. What are you doing?"

"Just the usual." Suzie waited for her husband to go on and when he didn't, she asked, "What's going on?"

"That's funny," he said. "I was about to ask you the same thing."

"Why?" Suzie asked. "What do you mean?"

"I'm coming home for lunch. We need to talk."

"Okay. I'll be here. You want to tell me what it is we need to talk about?"

"We'll talk when I get there."

Suzie heard the line disconnect. After pacing the floor, she grabbed her cell phone and called Vic.

"Vic, it's me. I may have a problem. Tommy just called and he's upset. He's coming home for lunch to talk."

"Why are you calling me?"

"Because he wouldn't tell me why he was upset. I'm scared, Vic."

"You sound pretty rattled. What are you scared about?"

"He must have learned something about our problem. Have you told anyone?"

"No, Suzie, and you're jumping to conclusions. Why don't you calm down and wait until you learn what Tom's upset about before going ballistic?"

"Okay, okay," she said. "I just wish all of this would come to an end. I don't want David and his problems interfering with my life anymore."

"Yeah. I hear that. This should be the end of it once he serves his time for the coke. The cops can't pin those murders on us."

Suzie loudly exhaled. "Yeah, you're right."

"I've got to get back to work," Vic said before hanging up the phone.

Ten minutes later, Suzie heard Tom's car pull into the driveway. She opened the front door to greet him.

"Hi, honey."

Tom walked past Suzie and into the house without responding. Suzie closed the front door and followed him into the den. She watched her husband walk across the room and stare out the bay window.

"What's wrong, honey?" she asked.

Tom responded without turning around. "I need to know what's going on."

"What do you mean?"

"You've been on edge lately, Suzie. Nervous about something. You gave up smoking because we thought it would be best for the kids. Now you're lighting up five or six times every evening, and I'm guessing several more times during the day." Tom turned around and faced his wife. "Are you having an affair?"

Suzie leaned back against the door frame. "No, Tommy. Why would you even think that? I admit that I've been nervous lately, and I probably should have mentioned something before now." Her eyes teared up. "It's just that a month ago, my friend Shirley learned that she has breast cancer."

Tom remained silent as he walked to the desk and sat down. "Go on."

"I'm sorry about the smoking. I guess I've been thinking so much about Shirley that I hadn't noticed. I agree it's not good for the kids. I'll stop."

Tom picked up a small paperweight on the desk and turned it around in his hand as though the action helped him to think. "Who's Vic, Suzie?"

"Vic?" she asked.

"Yes, Vic. The guy you've been calling and texting."

When Suzie started to talk, Tom interrupted. "Don't pretend you don't know who I'm talking about. He sent you a text while you were in the shower last night."

Suzie walked to a chair and sat down. "I saw the text. He was just asking me to call. You're right in that there is something going on, but it's not what you think. There is no other man. You're all I want and need, Tommy. You should know that."

Tom's expression was unchanged as he stared into Suzie's eyes. "Tell me about Vic."

"He's someone I've known since high school. I hadn't heard from him in years, and then out of the blue, I received his text a couple of weeks ago. Another guy we both knew in school has gone over the edge and is now in jail for selling drugs. Vic just wanted to know if we should visit him and persuade him to get clean." Suzie looked at her Tommy with pleading eyes. "I know now that I should have said something about it, but it just didn't seem that important, and my mind has been on Shirley."

Tom sat down at the desk. "Why would you even consider visiting some guy you knew in high school who's now in jail?"

"Well, our families were close. We're kind of like cousins the way we all grew up together."

"Cousins?" Tom asked. "I thought I knew all of your family. Why have I never heard of him before?"

Tears rolled down Suzie's cheeks. "I've been embarrassed to tell you about him. He's been a problem for a long time."

Tom stood up, walked around the desk, and put his arm around his wife's shoulders. "I'm sorry for jumping to conclusions. I should have just asked for an explanation. Will you forgive me?"

Suzie stood, hugged Tom, and kissed him. "Of course, darling, it was an honest mistake. I'll let Vic know that I'm not going to the jail with him."

Tom took a tissue from the box on the desk and wiped away his wife's tears. "I love you, Suzie."

Suzie smiled. "Love you too, Tommy."

As her husband drove away, Suzie picked up her phone and tapped in Vic's number.

CHAPTER TWELVE

Patty and Rick were at their desks early when a call came over the scanner. It was dispatch with an alert that a gas station convenience store had just been robbed. Brad and Pete were on patrol and responded immediately. Rick put down his coffee cup and Patty set her pencil aside. Eight minutes later they were at the scene and saw Brad approaching with a big smile on his face.

"What's going on?" Patty asked Brad as he held out a piece of paper. Patty looked at the note and handed it to Rick.

Rick read it and smiled. "An appointment reminder for his next PO visit. He's to meet this afternoon with PO Heart."

"Must have dropped it as he ran out," said Brad.

"Well, this will be one of the easy ones to solve," Patty said. "Call Heart and let her know what happened. Rick and I will go back to the station and interview him when she brings him in."

Rick was still smiling when they got back in the car.

"Have you had calls like this before?" Patty asked.

"Close. I once arrested a guy in an attempted burglary. He had dropped his wallet in the act. But as funny as that was, dropping an appointment card with your PO trumps all."

Patty smiled. "So, changing the subject, how'd your date with Barbara go?"

Rick looked up at Patty and paused before answering. "It was okay."

Patty nodded. "Oh, well that's good, I guess. So, are you going out again?"

Rick smiled, and Patty quickly spoke again before he could respond. "Oh, never mind. It really isn't my business anyway. I just wondered if you two were going to try and make it work again. You know, whether she has time for you and her business?"

Rick looked out the window. "That's still a concern of mine. She says her schedule isn't as hectic. We just had dinner and it went okay."

"Oh," said Patty "Well, that's nice."

Patty's cell phone rang, and she glanced at caller ID. "It's Doc Miller," she said to Rick. "Hi, Doc. How's your day going?"

"Pretty good, Patty, and yours is about to get a lot better. If Rick's there, you may want to put your call on speaker."

"He's here and listening. I've got you on speaker."

"Hi, Doc," Rick said. "The lab find something on the toothbrush or razor for our female victim?"

"Better than that," said the doctor. "I just heard from the lab, and they've got fingerprints for your victims."

Rick had pulled into the parking lot, where he turned off the engine and looked at Patty in disbelief. "Fingerprints?" he asked. "How? We saw their mummified hands, and they were clearly too dried out to provide prints."

Doc Miller laughed into the phone. "Oh, ye of little faith. Let me explain. They used a technique that's fairly unknown and not often called for. The victims' hands were soaked for a couple of days to moisten the skin, after which the tech cut the skin around each finger and then from the hand. She wrapped the moistened skin around her own gloved finger and rolled a print."

"Wow!" Patty exclaimed. "I've never heard of that before."

"It's beyond my experience," said Rick. "This is great!"

"When can you send the prints over?" asked Patty. "AFIS may find a match if either of our victims are in the system."

"I knew you'd want them as soon as possible," said the doctor, "My assistant is taking care of it. Give her an hour."

"That's amazing, Doc," said Patty.

Rick agreed. "Let the lab techs know we're in awe of their skills."

"You're both welcome. I'll pass on your words of appreciation. They'll continue to work on the DNA match from the toothbrush and razor, but the fingerprints may give you an ID a lot sooner."

"We need sooner," said Patty.

"You two stay safe out there," said the doctor. "You're looking for some dangerous people."

"Always," said Rick. "Thanks again, Doc."

Patty disconnected the call, and they walked to their office. "It never ceases to amaze me how far science has advanced during the time I've been a cop."

"I know what you mean," said Rick. "It sure makes our jobs easier."

Patty looked at the fingerprints she'd taken off the fax machine. "I'll let the LT know about this. He might be able to run them through the system on a fast track."

"While you do that, I could reschedule appointments with June's teachers. Do you want to go tomorrow if I can set it up?"

"Sure," said Patty before walking out of the room.

"Hello, O'Toole," the lieutenant greeted her as she stopped at his office door. "What have you got?"

Patty showed the faxed printout and explained how the lab was able to come up with fingerprints for both victims. "Have you heard of this technique before?" she asked.

"I read about it not too long ago. But I've never known of a case where it was used until now."

"Rick and I were wondering if you could do something for us."

"What's that?"

"We need to have these run through AFIS as soon as possible. Any chance you could expedite the process for us?"

"Possibly," said the lieutenant. "I'll let you know."

"Thanks, LT."

Patty returned to her desk to find Rick on the phone. Rather than sit down, she visited the break room, put several cookies on a couple of napkins, and set one napkin on the end of Rick's desk.

Rick finished his call and looked up. "Is this a celebratory gesture for the gift of prints?"

"It is. That and the fact that the LT is going to try to fast-track our AFIS search."

"I knew he'd come through," said Rick. "Now, changing the subject. I was able to schedule appointments with two teachers tomorrow, and I'm waiting to hear back from a third."

"That will work for me." Patty glanced at her watch. "My stomach's growling."

"It is. I can hear it from here. How about Blue Water? All of this excitement has made me hungry too, and they have a Reuben and fries with my name on it."

"Okay. Let's take my car so that I can fill the tank while we're out."

The restaurant was crowded when the detectives walked in. They were shown to a table with a large grass umbrella.

"I like the umbrellas and lights," said Patty. "Makes me think of Hawaii."

Rick's response was a smile.

Their meal choices arrived not long after they ordered. They had begun eating when a couple walked up to the table.

"May we help you?" Patty asked.

"I hope so," the woman answered.

"We're interrupting their lunch," said the husband, tugging on his wife's arm. "Let's just go sit down."

It's okay," said Patty. "Is there a problem, ma'am?"

The woman looked up at her husband and then back to Patty. "Well, I don't exactly know. This morning I got a call from someone claiming to be from the IRS. He said we have a $12,000 state refund coming, but we owe $3,000 on our federal income taxes which must be paid first. He wants us to mail in the $3,000, and he gave us the address to mail it to. I thought at first that it might be one of those scams I've heard about, but this man was quite helpful."

"They can't do anything about that," said the husband taking his wife's arm. "Let's go eat."

The woman pulled her arm away and continued to talk. "He knew our names including our middle initials. I just don't know what to do. We could sure use the extra $9,000."

Patty glanced at Rick and then looked up to the couple. "It's a scam. Don't send the money. The IRS doesn't demand payment of back taxes over the phone."

"So I should just ignore it?" asked the woman.

"Yes," said Patty. "If they call again, you can ask them to send their request to you in writing. Hang up if they ask for your address. If you receive something in writing from what seems like the IRS, bring it into the police station and we'll look at it for you."

The woman smiled up at her husband and then at Patty and Rick. "Thank you so much, officer."

"You're welcome," said Patty.

"Now can we go eat?" asked the husband.

Patty went back to eating her chicken Caesar salad and noticed Rick had finished his sandwich.

"Told you I was hungry," he said.

"You did. I'll get a to-go box and we can head back to the station. Does the number of scams going on all the time surprise you?"

"No. These scams wouldn't continue if it weren't for the fact that a lot of people fall for them and that makes a few other people wealthy."

"You'd think they'd get bored just making robo calls all day," said Patty.

"They're probably making a lot more with their scams than we do working. Money can create a lot of tolerance for monotony."

After lunch, the detectives gassed up Patty's car and started back to the station. As Patty drove, Rick quickly turned to get a better look at the small truck they'd just passed.

"Someone you know?" asked Patty.

"Slow down," said Rick. "I want to get a better look at the back window."

Patty slowed down enough for the small truck to pass them. Rick tapped a number into his cell phone."

"What's up?" asked Patty.

Before Rick could respond, the person he called came on the line.

"Hey, Pete," Rick said. "Do you still have that small black pick-up truck?"

"Yeah."

"Where is it right now?"

"Parked in my driveway at home. Why?"

"Because it just passed Patty and me on Chetco."

"Why do you think it's mine?"

"It has your Made in America sticker on the back window, and a small dent on the right rear bumper."

Patty could hear Pete hollering into his phone. "Son-of-a-gun. I'm at the station now. Nail him and hold him until I get there. I'm on my way."

Patty lit up the car, turned around, and took off after the guy. Thirty minutes later, the driver was locked up in a holding cell, and Pete was in the break room with a cup of coffee. Rick walked in carrying both his and Patty's coffee cups.

"I still can't believe my truck was stolen from in front of my own house. I live in a good neighborhood."

"Haven't you heard?" asked Rick. "Bad things can happen to good people. You're lucky you got it back in one piece."

"I may not have if you hadn't spotted it. Did I tell you thanks?"

"You did," said Rick. "And now you owe me."

"Owe you what?"

Rick smiled. "Nothing specific that I can think of right now. I'll let you know if something comes up."

"Okay. I owe you as long as it's within reason."

Rick nodded, filled the coffee cups, and grabbed a few cookies before returning to his desk. He gave Patty's coffee to her. "You want a cookie?"

"No. I'm holding out for a chocolate old-fashioned doughnut."

"Kind of late in the day for doughnuts."

Patty laughed. "This said by a guy holding a handful of cookies."

Rick looked down at the cookies in his hand. "Well, cookies are made to be eaten at any time of day."

Patty smiled. "Of course." She took a sip of her coffee and put the cup down. "You know, that's two lucky breaks we've had in one day. I've heard that good things happen in threes. Do you believe that?"

Rick shrugged his shoulders. Before he could say anything, Patty's cell phone rang.

"Detective O'Toole."

"Hello, Detective O'Toole, this is your mother."

"Hi, Mom. How's your day going?"

"It's been interesting. I'm calling because I reported to jury duty this morning and was accepted to serve as a juror on today's trial. We agreed upon a verdict before five."

"Well, that's efficient. What was the alleged crime?"

"The defendant was accused of starting a garbage can on fire behind one of the city buildings."

"You must have had some solid evidence for the entire jury to agree upon a verdict within a few hours."

"It was enough. We had two body-cam videos to watch and the security camera video from the public building. One body-cam video was from the evening before the event when the defendant was stopped and questioned by an officer. Before the end of the video, the defendant told the officer that he was going to start a fire."

"Well, I call that some pretty good evidence, Mom. What did you see on the building security film?"

"It showed the defendant on the day of the crime leaving the building through the back door and walking around the fenced yard area toward the side of the building where the garbage cans are. He was outside of the camera range for about ten minutes and then was seen walking back into the building. The fire was noticed not long after that."

"And the second body-cam video?"

"That was taken later in the day after the fire was put out. Two officers approached the defendant, who was hanging out with another guy. The defendant pretended to be unable to understand what the officers were asking."

"Did he slip up?"

"Well, not exactly. He was acting really weird. But the other guy yelled out to the defendant that he wasn't the one who called the cops on him."

"Do you think he was capable of understanding what was being asked?"

"Oh, yeah. He understood. In court he was completely different and looked embarrassed when he saw himself on the video screen."

"After all that," Patty said, "why did it take you more than a couple of hours to agree upon a verdict?"

"We had two jurors who were coming up with one excuse after the other for the guy as to why he walked around the building where the fire was started. One woman said that the defendant may have just been down on his luck and needed some time to himself. She said he may have walked around the back of the building to think about how hard his life had been and that he just needed a break. Another said he may have just walked around the building to smoke a cigarette."

"So how'd you and the others handle that?"

"Not so well. One juror blurted out that he knew the defendant was guilty as hell, and that he wasn't leaving until we'd decided on a conviction."

"That wasn't very helpful," Patty said. "How did you and the others respond?"

"The first thing we did was to watch the videos again. After that, one of the two women changed her mind and decided the defendant was guilty. She said that she hadn't previously heard the defendant tell the officer that he was going to start a fire."

"And then?" Patty asked.

"Well, then I went over a few things. I said that we needed to remind ourselves why we were there. That it wasn't our responsibility to make an oral judgement based upon the defendant's life experience."

"That was good, Mom."

"Then I repeated what we were told before deliberating: that there are two kinds of evidence, actual and circumstantial. I reminded them that our case was one of circumstantial evidence and that all we needed to do was use common sense in reviewing the evidence. We didn't have to see the defendant commit the crime, nor did anyone else."

"Did your explanation make a difference?"

"It did. They were all ready to convict except one, and she repeated her suggestion that he may have walked to the back of the building to smoke a cigarette."

"What made her change her mind?"

"One of the other jurors spoke up and said that if he truly had walked around the back of the building to smoke a cigarette, his attorney would have used that as his defense. She thought about that and agreed to convict."

"I think you missed your calling, Mom. You should have been an attorney."

"You know, dear, I think I would have enjoyed being a contract attorney, but I wouldn't want to litigate. One day in court and I'm exhausted."

CHAPTER THIRTEEN

The next morning the detectives left Brookings for the two-hour drive to College of the Redwoods, where Rick had rescheduled three appointments. As they drove along the coast Rick asked, "How are Bill and your mom?"

"They're doing well. Thanks for asking. Bill's tests are all coming out great, and my mom is staying busy. She just completed her civic duty by serving on a jury trial that resulted in a conviction."

"That must be satisfying. Are they planning another cruise soon?"

"Not a cruise. Mom says they'll see more of the US on their next trip. They'll travel by train and luxury coach."

"Great way to travel," said Rick. "What about Bill's gambling needs?"

"He's slowed down since being sick, but I'm sure he won't stop completely. They'll just take shorter trips."

The detectives arrived on campus and parked in front of the Admissions office. Inside, they were directed to a room with a table and several chairs, offered coffee, and left waiting for their first appointment.

"It's a beautiful campus," said Patty, "and large for a two-year college."

Rick was standing in front of the window looking out. "Historic-looking."

The door opened and a young man walked in. "Hello. I'm Dave Elders, June Deboe's chemistry teacher."

"We're Detectives O'Toole and Starker," said Patty. "Thank you for taking the time to meet with us."

"Sure. I'm sorry to learn that June is missing. What can I do for you?"

"When is the last time you saw June?" Patty asked.

"About five months ago. She just quit coming to class."

Patty gave a puzzled look. "Didn't you think that odd? Odd enough to want to look into it?"

"This is a college campus, Detective. Not a high school. The students here are adults. They can legally come and go as they please. Whether they attend enough classes and can earn the grades they need to graduate is up to them."

Rick stepped forward. "We have reason to believe that June was using and possibly selling drugs. Do you have any knowledge of this?"

"I'd heard that she might be using. I didn't know about the selling."

"How did you hear about her using?" asked Rick.

"June began missing classes after having been a pretty good student. I asked a couple other students in my class if they knew what the problem was, and they told me what was going on."

"When was this?" Patty asked.

"About the time she quit coming to class."

"Are the students who told you about June still in your class?"

"They are."

"We'll need their names," said Patty.

Rick looked up from his notepad. "Did you hear anything about where she was buying the drugs? Was it on campus?"

"I'm sure drugs are available on this campus just like they are on most college campuses, but no one told me who she was buying from."

"I understand," said Patty. "Thank you for your time."

"No problem. I hope that you find her."

After Mr. Elders left the room, Patty and Rick checked their cell phones for messages and calls.

"Let's hope the next two teachers know more than he did," said Rick.

"We can hope," said Patty.

Several minutes later the door opened, and an older woman stepped in.

"Hello, Detectives," she said pleasantly. "I'm Vera Adams, June Deboe's business teacher. I understand that you have some questions about June."

"We do," said Patty. "I'm Detective O'Toole and this is Detective Starker. When was the last time you saw June?"

"I anticipated that question when I was asked to meet with you. I saw her three months ago, shortly after she'd stopped coming to class."

"Tell us about the most recent meeting," said Patty.

"It was the end of the day. I saw her in the school parking lot as I walked to my car."

"What was she doing?"

"She was talking with another woman. I don't think I'd have paid any attention, but their voices were loud, as though they were arguing."

"What, besides the volume of their voices, gave you the impression they were arguing?"

"I don't remember exactly. But June is generally a soft-spoken person, and she sounded as though she were mad at the woman."

"Was the other woman a student?" asked Rick.

"She wasn't in any of my classes, and she didn't carry a book bag. I got the impression that she was there just to meet up with June."

"You say she didn't have a book bag. Did she have anything in her hands?" asked Patty.

Vera brought her hand up to her face and began tapping her fingers against her chin as she thought. "You know, she did have something in her hand. It was a bag. I guess I didn't think much of it because it looked like a lunch bag."

"Did you notice if she gave the bag to June?"

"I didn't. I got into my car and left."

"So," asked Patty, "you never saw the other woman before that day?"

"I didn't get a close look at her. If she'd been on campus, she would have melded in with the other students. Though it did look to me like she was older than most of our students."

"What made her look older?" Patty asked.

"The way she dressed. Like someone with more money than most college students."

"Okay, Ms. Adams," said Patty. "That's all we have for now. Thank you for your time. If you think of anything else, please give one of us a call."

"Happy to help if it moves you closer to finding June. I hope she's okay."

The third teacher walked in as Vera left.

"You must be Robert Brown," Patty said.

"I am. And you must be the detectives looking for June Deboe."

"We are," said Patty. "When was the last time you saw June?"

"She hasn't come to class in about three months, but I saw her on campus not long after that."

"What were the circumstances when you last saw her?"

"I walked past her during the lunch hour. She was in the courtyard with a couple of other students."

"Did you know the other students?" asked Patty.

"One of them. He's in my afternoon art class."

"We'd like his name and contact information."

"I can give you his name. Admissions will have his contact information."

"Could you hear what June and the other students were talking about?"

"I really wasn't paying attention, and frankly I didn't care. I was a little pissed that she just dropped out of my class without talking to me first. I knew she was using drugs and I'd cautioned her about it a few months prior."

"How'd you know she was using?" Patty asked.

"Another student told me. He said June was buying drugs on campus and that he'd heard she was also trying to sell them."

"Did the other student know who was selling the drugs to June?"

"Just that it was some woman who'd periodically show up on campus."

"We need to talk with the student who told you about the drugs," said Patty.

"That would be Jeff. He just finished his class with me. I'll ask Admissions to locate him."

"When you spoke with June, what did she say?"

"She said what they all say. Didn't want to talk about it. When I asked if she was selling, she told me it wasn't any of my business. I told her it was my business and that if I learned of someone she'd sold drugs to, I'd go to the authorities."

"How did she respond to that?" asked Patty.

"She said she wasn't selling anything. Just using a little herself. I asked if she had any idea what she was getting herself into, and how her using drugs would affect her life."

"And her response?" asked Rick.

"For the first time, she paused before answering me. She told me she didn't plan on doing it much longer and asked that I leave her alone. I remember seeing tears in her eyes when she finished talking."

Patty glanced at Rick, who nodded and put the small note tablet into his pocket.

She turned back to Robert. "That's all the questions we have for you now. We'll need the contact information for both students you mentioned. Since your class just let out, could you stop by Admissions and ask where we'd find Jeff now?"

"Sure. I'll ask that he be sent here if they locate him."

Twenty minutes passed before Jeff Woods arrived. While waiting for Woods, Patty and Rick discussed what they'd heard from the teachers and their plan for interviewing the three students. At nineteen, Jeff was one of the older students. He was dressed in blue jeans washed often enough to have faded the brand name printed across the back.

"Are you Jeff?" asked Patty.

"Yeah. The office said you have some questions about June Deboe."

"That's right. Please have a seat."

Woods sat down, and Patty began the questioning. "When was the last time you saw June?"

"I don't know. Maybe two months ago."

"What were the circumstances of your meeting with her?"

Jeff looked around the room. "I'd been talking with a fellow student from Mr. Brown's class, and June and some other girl walked up to me."

"What did June want?"

"She asked me how class was going. I told her it was good."

"Did you ask her why she quit attending?"

"Yeah, I did. She said she wasn't much interested in school anymore. Said she was working."

"Did she say what kind of work she was doing?"

"Not at first. But then I said that I'd heard she was making money selling drugs."

"And what did she say to that?"

"She wanted to know where I'd heard that she was selling, and I told her that everyone knew. That a few of the students had seen her talking with some woman on campus who was giving her drugs to sell. Then I looked at the girl June was with and asked if she was one of June's customers."

"And was she?" Patty asked.

"The girl didn't answer."

Patty and Rick sat quietly, and Patty nodded for Jeff to continue.

"June seemed surprised at what I knew. Then she got mad. She said she'd only sold a couple of times and was no longer doing it. Said that I could spread that information around. Then she and the girl walked away."

Rick looked up from the notes he'd been taking. "Have you seen this woman who students think was selling June the drugs?"

"Only from across the campus. Maybe two or three times."

"Can you describe her?" Rick asked.

"She has blond hair that hangs down to her shoulders. She was in blue jeans. I don't remember much else."

"Did you see her well enough," asked Rick, "to tell if she was about the same age as you?"

"No, not really. I figured she wasn't a student because I hadn't seen her on campus other than those few times with June. But I heard from others that the woman was older than most of us. What do you think happened to June?"

"We don't know," said Patty. "That's what we're trying to find out. You've been very helpful, Jeff, and I have one last question. Do you know the girl who was with June when June spoke with you?"

"I don't know her personally, but I can find out who she is."

Patty and Rick gave their business cards to the young man. "Please call one of us when you know her name. We'll want to talk with her."

"Well," said Rick after the student left, "can't say we know a whole lot more than when we arrived."

"No, but we may learn a lot by talking with that student who was with June. If she's a drug user, there's a chance she met this mystery woman."

A knock at the door caused Rick and Patty to stop their conversation. Dave Elders was standing at the door with a young woman.

"This is Celeste," he said. "She's in the same class that June had been attending and may be able to help. She'd like for me to stay."

Patty made eye contact with Rick and then looked back at Elders. "It's okay, if you can remain silent and let Celeste answer our questions."

He nodded and then sat down, motioning to Celeste to do the same.

Patty started the questioning. "We're detectives from Brookings. Do you know why we're here?"

"You're looking for June," she said.

"That's right. When did you last see her?"

"About two months ago."

"Please tell us about that," said Patty.

Celeste looked sheepishly at the floor and then over to her teacher, who tipped his head toward Patty as if telling Celeste to go ahead.

"I bought some drugs from June."

"What kind of drugs?"

"Mostly meth and coke."

Patty glanced again at Rick and then sat forward in her chair. "How long had you been buying from her?"

"Are you going to arrest me for buying the drugs?"

"No. We're here to find out what happened to June."

"Okay. I bought from June three times. I don't use all the time, just when I get really depressed."

"Did you ever see where June bought the drugs she sold to you?"

Celeste slid back and forth in her chair. "Yeah. June bought them from a woman who came to the campus."

"Did you meet this woman?"

"No, but I saw her and asked June who she was."

"Did June give you her name?"

"Not exactly, but I heard it. When I saw her a couple of months ago, June and I were talking and she suddenly said she had to go meet with Suzie. When I looked where June was walking, it was to the car of the drug woman."

Rick continued taking notes as Patty moved on with her questioning.

"Can you describe her for us?"

"She had blond, shoulder-length hair, wore blue jeans and a jacket."

"What was your overall impression of her? Did she look like she could be a student?"

Celeste paused and thought about the question. "No. She was dressed nicer than most of the students. Her jeans didn't look worn and her jacket was leather. She wore a scarf around her neck too."

"What color were the scarf and jacket?" Patty asked.

"The jacket was black. I don't really remember the scarf very well, but it might have been yellow. Yes, I think it was yellow."

"Did you see her leave? Get into a car?"

"No. When they were done, June walked back over to me, and I bought some stuff from her."

"Have you seen this woman since the last time you were with June?"

"No."

"You're being very helpful, Celeste. Just a couple more questions. What was June's behavior like when you saw her that last time? Was it different from earlier times when you'd meet up?"

Celeste furrowed her eyebrows and thought for a minute. "She seemed bothered by something. Like she wasn't happy to sell to me. She quickly took my money and walked away."

"Did she say anything about why she was unhappy?" Patty asked.

"Not exactly," said Celeste. "She told me I'd have to buy my drugs from someone else after that. Then she just left."

Patty looked at Rick and he closed his notepad. She looked up at Mr. Elders and Celeste. "Thank you both. If you think of anything else or talk with anyone who spoke with June within the past three months, please let us know."

Celeste started out the door and then turned to Patty and Rick. "I hope you find out what happened to her. She was always nice to me."

Rick and Patty gathered their things in preparation to leave.

"Well, now we've got a name to go with the blond hair," said Rick.

"And we know she's probably not been on campus since June told some of the students that she was going to stop selling. This is looking more and more like whatever happened to her is a retaliation for no longer being willing to sell."

Rick agreed. "Drug dealers don't like buyers who want out after establishing a relationship."

CHAPTER FOURTEEN

Rick and Patty were halfway back to Brookings when Patty's cell phone rang.

"Hey, Brad."

"Hi, Patty. I've got good news and bad news."

"What's the good news?"

"We've got a match on AFIS to both victims."

Patty put her cell phone on speaker. "I've just put you on speaker so that Rick can hear. Go ahead."

"We've got hits on the prints for both victims."

"Both of them?" Rick asked.

"Your male victim was arrested twice for DUIIs, and your female had her prints taken eight months ago when she was caught stealing from her employer, a local lounge."

"An ID on both victims is good news," said Rick.

"Brad?" Patty asked.

"Yeah?"

"You said there was good news and bad news. So what's the bad news?"

"Your female victim is June Deboe."

There was a noticeable silence. A few moments later, Rick exhaled. "That means we can stop looking for her and direct our efforts toward finding her killer."

"You won't have to look far," Brad said. "The male victim's prints match those on the 1911 found in his hand. The gun was matched to both the casing found at the scene and the bullet recovered from the body."

"Okay," said Patty. "We now know the identity of our female victim, how she was killed, and who killed her. What's the ID on the male?"

"His name is Howard Heising and he was thirty-five years old. At the time of his last DUII, about nine years ago, he was a resident of Grants Pass."

"Thanks, Brad," said Patty. "Rick and I will contact June's parents."

"Glad I could help."

Patty disconnected the call and sat silently with Rick as they drove north for fifteen minutes through the redwoods.

"I'll call the Deboes," said Patty, "and ask them to meet us at the station in an hour. That will give us a little time to prepare for them."

"Okay," said Rick.

"This is going to be difficult."

"It is," agreed Rick.

* * *

The Deboes slowly lowered themselves into the chairs across from Patty and Rick. Patty spoke quietly. "Mr. and Mrs. Deboe, it is with great sadness that we let you know that the woman whose death we've been investigating is your daughter June."

Mrs. Deboe stood up suddenly, faced the back wall, slapped the palms of her hands against the wall, and let out a loud, guttural groan. Mr. Deboe stood up and put his arms around his wife's shoulders. The two of them just stood there as time stopped for them and life as they'd known it ceased to exist. When they turned back, large tears escaped from his sunken eyes and slowly rolled down his face as he helped place his wife in her chair. When she looked up at her husband, it was with pleading eyes, as though she wanted him to tell her it wasn't true. He put his arm around her and held her to his chest.

Patty's eyes began to tear up as she imagined the horror of losing a child. The possibility of no longer having her Becky was incomprehensible.

"Can we see her?" asked Mr. Deboe.

Patty looked at Rick and he responded. "I'm sorry. There's been too much time since she died."

Mrs. Deboe pushed away from her husband and faced Rick. "I need to see my baby. Where do we go? I want to see June!"

Mr. Deboe looked at Patty. She saw the helplessness in his hollow eyes and slowly moved her head from side to side. The broken man then looked at Rick as though he couldn't comprehend what was happening.

"I'm sorry," Rick said again. "The body no longer bears any resemblance to June. It's best you remember her as the beautiful, loving daughter she was."

"How do you know for sure it's her?" asked Mr. Deboe.

Patty momentarily glanced at Rick and then responded to the grieving father. "The medical examiner's office was able to use a unique forensic procedure. I'll explain it to you later, if you like. Right now, I'd like for one of our officers to take you both home. We'll have an officer drop your car off, if that's okay. Do you have a family member or friend who can stay with you for the next few days?"

"We have a neighbor," he said. "I'll call when we get home. You can have an officer drop the car off. Here's the key."

Rick stepped out of the room for a minute and came back with Pete. "This is Officer Chekowsky. He'll take you home. You'll want to plan a funeral service. Do you have a preference in chapels?"

"The local one is fine. Can you have them call me?"

"We'll do that," Patty said. "One of us will be in touch within the next few days. Don't hesitate to call if you have any questions."

The Deboes stood up, and Pete walked with them out the door.

Rick, with anger in his eyes, turned toward Patty. "We've got to find this Suzie woman and put a stop to her dealing to kids."

"We will. Let's talk with the brother again and find out if he knows a Suzie. Chances are that if she was selling drugs to June, Suzie also knows June's killer."

Walking back to their office Rick took a detour into the kitchen and then joined Patty.

"You're empty-handed," she said as he sat down at his desk.

"That's because there's nothing to eat. I think our volunteer who bakes cookies is falling down on the job."

Patty smiled. "Good thing you had your maple bar this morning."

Rick paused a moment. "Not too long ago I'd have needed a drink."

"Does the urge come often?" Patty asked.

"Every day, and sometimes several times a day."

"I'm proud of you, Rick, for being as strong as you are."

"I just know to take it one day at a time. And I rely heavily on my higher power to keep me strong."

Patty found herself wanting to put her arms around Rick and hold him. He had been through so much.

Rick broke their glance and looked down at this file. "We need to talk with Dorisko about our campus drug dealer. You going to call PO Lincoln?"

"Right now," said Patty. "Okay if we drive up there tomorrow?"

"Yeah. Let's make it an early appointment if possible so that we can get back here before six. There's a game on TV I'd like to watch."

Patty called David Dorisko's parole officer to give her an update and was glad when it didn't go to voice mail.

"PO Lincoln, this is Detective O'Toole. We've identified our double-homicide victims and have a lead on a possible suspect. We'd like to interview Dorisko tomorrow at eleven. We believe he may know our suspect."

"No problem. I'll notify the jail."

Patty ended the call and stood up. "I need to let the LT know about the identifications. You want to make a list of what we've got thus far?"

"Sure," said Rick. "I'll add to what I've already got going."

In the lieutenant's office Patty explained how the interviews led to a Suzie as the provider of drugs to June, and then she spoke of meeting with the Deboes.

"Does it ever get easy?" she asked.

"No, and that's as it should be. The day you feel nothing when telling a parent that their child has died is the day you need to resign."

"It's such a helpless feeling at a time when you know it's your words that are causing such extreme pain."

"You're not helpless, O'Toole. You and Rick can solve this case and learn why June Deboe was killed. There will never be what we refer to as closure about the loss of their child, but finding the reason for June's death and seeing that those responsible are punished will close the book on the legal interference in their lives, allowing them to fully grieve their loss."

Patty listened to her superior and nodded her head. "Thanks."

The lieutenant sat back in his chair. "Find the girl who hung out with June. She should provide more information on this Suzie suspect."

"We're working on it," said Patty as she left the office and started back to her desk. Her message light was blinking, and she listened to the call.

"Detective O'Toole, this is Jeff Woods. You and another detective interviewed me at the college and asked if I could locate the student who was with June the last time I saw her. Well, I know who she is. Call me back if you still want her name."

Patty tapped in the number and Woods picked up. "Mr. Woods, this is Detective O'Toole. You've located the girl you saw with June Deboe?"

"Yeah. Her name is Gina Kibble and she's a student here."

"Have you spoken with her?"

"Yeah, I saw her yesterday on campus and asked her what her name is. I told her that you needed to talk with her about June. She was pretty shook up."

"Did you tell her anything else?" asked Patty.

"No. Just your name and that you wanted to talk with her."

"Thank you, Jeff. We appreciate your help."

Patty called the Admissions desk at the college, got a phone number for Gina Kibble, and called it.

"Hello. Gina Kibble?"

"Yes. Who's this?"

"Gina, this is Detective O'Toole. My partner and I are investigating the death of June Deboe. We'd like to ask you some questions and would prefer to meet with you."

"Did you say 'death'? June is dead?"

Patty put the call on speaker phone and caught Rick's attention before continuing.

"She is." Patty waited for a response from Gina and, when there wasn't one, continued. "Can you meet us in Brookings Thursday morning?"

"No. I'm in Redding, and I don't want to meet with you. They'll find out."

"Okay, Gina. I'll ask my questions over the phone for now. I have you on speaker phone so that my partner can participate in our call. Do you know anyone who would have wanted to harm June?"

"No. I can't believe she's dead. How did she die?"

"She was murdered," Patty said.

Patty heard a gasp from Gina. "Oh, no," she said. "They really killed her."

"Who killed her?" asked Patty.

"Oh, my God!"

"Gina, please answer my questions. Who killed her?"

"The dealers June got her drugs from."

"Why do you think they killed her?"

"Because she wanted to quit. She told Suzie that she was done selling and using drugs. June even tried to get me to stop. Suzie told June it didn't work that way."

"Gina, this is Detective Starker. Have you met Suzie?"

"I did meet her once. June and I were leaving the campus and a car pulled up. It was Suzie with some guy in the car. She hollered at June, and after they talked for a few minutes, June waved me over to the car. She introduced me to Suzie."

"Do you know why Suzie wanted to meet you?"

"I got the feeling Suzie was going to ask me to sell for her."

"What happened after you spoke?"

"She gave June some drugs in exchange for June's cash. Then Suzie and the guy left."

"Do you remember the car?" Patty asked.

"A little. It was a pretty nice car. Dark blue."

"Four doors?" Patty asked.

"Yes, like an SUV. It looked expensive."

"What about the guy in the car with Suzie? What did he look like?"

"He looked about the same age as her and he had black hair."

"Was his hair long?"

"Kind of. He wore it pushed behind his ears."

"What about a beard or mustache?" asked Patty.

Gina thought for a moment. "I remember him bringing his hand up and running it over a beard. That was all."

Patty covered the phone mouthpiece and whispered to Rick. "Dorisko?"

"Could be," he said quietly.

"Have you seen him since that day?"

"No."

"Did June know who he was?" asked Patty.

"I asked her, and she didn't know. She said she'd never seen him before."

"Gina," Patty said, "you've seen how drug use can make a person's face look hard. Did the man look like he was a drug user?"

"I don't remember thinking that."

"Can you remember anything about his clothes?"

"Not really. I only saw them for a minute. And I was scared."

"Okay," said Patty. "Is there anything else you can remember?"

"No. Well, yes. I don't know if it's important, but there was a child's car seat in the back of the car. The kind for an older child. Not an infant. It struck me as odd, and I felt sorry for the child."

"I need to know, Gina," Patty asked. "Do you have any interest in selling drugs?"

"No! No, I don't want anything to do with it. I'm going to quit using too. I'm afraid they'll come after me next. I saw Suzie and that man. That's why I'm not going back to Eureka."

"Will you let us know if Suzie contacts you?"

"Yeah. Like I said, I don't want anything to do with her or her drugs."

"Okay. Thanks. That's all the questions we have for now."

Patty ended the call and tapped her pen on the desk. "So Suzie has a family."

"And an expensive car," Rick said. "All we need now is a last name."

* * *

The detectives left early to arrive at their appointment with David Dorisko by eleven.

They walked into the interview room to find Dorisko cuffed to the metal ring embedded into the table.

"Hello, Dorisko," said Rick. "We've got a few more questions to ask you. Do you recall your Miranda rights that your PO read to you?"

Dorisko ignored the question and remained silent as Rick took a small card from his pocket and read the Miranda rights. "Do you understand these rights?" Rick asked. "You can tell us to stop questioning you any time you want."

Hearing no comment, Patty stood up. "No sense in trying to eliminate him as a suspect," she said to Rick. "Let's leave him locked up."

Rick stood up to leave and Dorisko spoke. "Alright. Yes, I understand my rights. Go ahead and ask your questions."

The detectives took their seats, and Patty began the questioning. "We've learned about one of your friends."

Dorisko sat silently with an assured smirk on his face.

"Don't you want to know which one of your dealers it is?"

Dorisko shifted in his seat, and a slight look of fear showed in his eyes before he put his head down and stared at the table.

Rick slammed the palm of his hand down on the table, causing the frightened man to jump and look up. "I asked you a question. Which drug-dealing friend do you think we've learned about? This will keep you locked up for at least twenty years, and maybe for life as an accomplice to murder."

Rick's statement caught Dorisko's attention. "Murder? What are you talking about? I've got nothing to do with any murder."

"We've connected one of the victims found in your brother's storage unit to a drug dealer who dealt at a Eureka college."

Dorisko furrowed his brows as he processed what he'd just heard. "I don't know anything about a drug dealer at the college, or any murder."

"I think you do," said Rick. "I think you and Suzie know each other well."

The smirk disappeared from Dorisko's face as he squirmed again in his chair. He looked up at the ceiling and then across the table to Rick and Patty. "I don't know what you're talking about. I don't know any Suzie."

Rick sat back and exchanged a glance with Patty who took up the questioning.

"We know that you do, David. We have a witness who saw you and Suzie in her car at the college, talking with June Deboe."

Dorisko sat upright in his chair, leaning so that the front of the chair lifted on the back two legs. "I don't know who you're talking about," he said.

"How about your friend who makes beer?" asked Rick. "Tell us about him."

Dorisko's eyes looked frightened as they moved back and forth between Patty and Rick. "I don't have a friend who makes beer."

"Sure you do," said Rick. "You stashed his supplies in your brother's storage shed. Then hid the kilo in one of his containers."

"That's just some stuff that a friend gave me. I don't know what it's used for."

"You do," said Rick, "and you'd better start helping yourself or you'll be spending a long time on the inside. What's your friend's name?"

Dorisko looked down at the table.

Patty closed her notepad. "Okay, David. We've noted that you've refused to cooperate. You've spent a little time in prison. Most men don't want to return. But we're going to find out why June Deboe was killed, and if it's tied to your drugs, we'll make sure you never get out."

The detectives left Eugene for Brookings.

* * *

Suzie was enjoying a glass of white wine as she relaxed on one of the many lounge chairs set up on her back deck. It was 2:30 in the afternoon and she had twenty minutes before she'd leave to pick up the children from school. As she wiggled her bare toes in the warm sun her cell phone rang. With the glass in one hand, she picked up the cell phone with the other.

"Is this Suzie?" a voice asked.

"Who wants to know?" she asked.

"That's not important. I'm calling for Dorisko, and he says the cops were there today asking about you."

The wine glass hit the deck and shattered.

CHAPTER FIFTEEN

Patty arrived at the office and found Rick sitting at his desk eating a bacon-topped maple bar and staring out the window.

"What are you thinking about?" Patty asked.

Rick continued to stare. "Nothing."

"Nothing?" she asked.

"Nothing," he repeated.

"Well, that's not possible. There must be thoughts about something going on in your head. You can't just think about nothing."

Rick looked up at Patty and smiled. "Men can."

Patty stared back at him and then shook her head. "Well, I still question whether that's possible. The only time I'm thinking about nothing is when I'm sleeping. And even then, my mind isn't always quiet because I'm dreaming."

"I'm sorry," Rick said.

Patty's cell phone rang, interrupting the conversation. "Detective O'Toole." She listened to the caller and waved at Rick to get his attention. Rick sat back in his chair.

"Hello, Gerold. Just a minute. Detective Starker is here, and I'm going to put you on speaker phone. I want Detective Starker to also know that you've received a call from the guy who owns the beer equipment."

Rick sat up. "Gerold, what's this guy's name?"

"He didn't tell me."

"When did he call?"

"A few minutes ago. He said he wanted his beer equipment back, and I told him I couldn't get into the unit because of the murders."

"Have you ever met him?" Patty asked.

"I can't tell by his voice, but I may have met him at the party I told you about in Eugene."

"Did he seem to know about the murders?"

Gerold cleared his throat. "Yeah, he did. He said he had nothing to do with that and just wants his stuff."

"Hold on a minute," Patty said. She put her hand over the phone receiver and whispered to Rick. "We could set things up to meet the guy. Let's have Gerold call him back." Rick nodded.

"Gerold, we want to talk with this guy, and you can help us."

"What do you mean?"

"We want you to call the guy back and set up a time for him to meet you at the storage unit. Tell him you've got a friend who's a locksmith and will open the door for you."

"Uh, I don't think I want to do this. I don't want this guy angry at me."

"We're just going to talk with him," Rick said. "This might help us to eliminate him as a suspect. And the sooner we can narrow down the possible suspects, the sooner you'll have access to your storage unit. That's what you want. Right?"

"Yeah," he said. "Okay, I'll call him back. But this better not be a trick. My brother knows some pretty bad guys."

"Before you go," said Patty, "we need the guy's caller ID number from your cell phone, and the name of your cell phone provider."

Gerold gave her the information, and Patty ended the call. "While we're waiting on the call back, let's see what we can find on Howard Heising. Since no one's reported him missing, he's probably not from around here. There can't be too many people with his last name. I'll check the Oregon and California missing persons database if you want to check NaMus.gov."

Rick nodded and began tapping the deceased's name into the computer. Five minutes had passed when Patty's cell phone rang. "It's Dorisko."

Rick listened to Patty's side of the conversation.

"That's good. Two o'clock should work. We'll plan on showing up at about one-thirty so that we don't spook him by driving up when he does. We'll see you this afternoon."

"This," Patty said to Rick, "could be the break we need. I'll give the phone number and provider information to Brad. The provider may have a name for the cell number."

At one-thirty the detectives arrived at the storage facility and Gerold Dorisko's unit. Dorisko was leaning against the stucco exterior wall. They parked their car in the next aisle over so that it couldn't be seen, and Patty told him what to do. "We'll wait at the manager's office. You stay here so that he can see you when he arrives."

"Okay," said Dorisko. "I just hope he doesn't get angry with me."

At two o'clock the detectives continued to wait. Two cars had entered the facility, but the drivers of both cars went to different units where Rick could see them roll up their doors. Ten minutes later, the detectives saw Dorisko answer his cell phone and then start walking toward them.

"This doesn't look good," said Rick.

"A no-show," said Patty.

"He's changed his mind," Dorisko said as he approached. "Said it would be too easy for this to be a set-up, and he doesn't really need his equipment right now."

"What did you say?" asked Rick.

Dorisko shrugged his shoulders and looked down at his shoes. "What could I say? I'm scared after finding two dead people in my storage unit, so I told him no problem." He raised his head and looked at the detectives. "You need to find out who killed those people."

"Did he call you back after you set this up with him?" Patty asked.

"No. I didn't talk with him again until his call just now."

"Okay," said Patty. "Call us if he gets in touch with you again. And get his name."

Dorisko didn't answer but slowly nodded his head.

Patty and Rick returned to the office. "Let's continue our search for a relative of Heising," Patty said. "Someone must care enough to have reported him missing. You know, Rick, I've had only a few missing person cases. It's hard for me to wrap my mind around the fact that there are over six hundred thousand people reported missing each year."

"We had a lot of them in Boston. Thankfully, most of those reported missing are found alive and well. It's the tens of thousands who go missing for more than a year that cause cops a lot of heartburn. Websites like NamUs give us a much better chance of locating someone today than was the case not too long ago."

The detectives turned back to their respective searches, and within a few minutes Rick had a match. "He's here. I'll call and get family information."

"It's always reassuring when the system works," said Patty.

Rick input the required information into the online contact form. "This should put us a lot closer to learning what our victim had to do with June Deboe and why he killed her."

A few minutes passed before a new email showed up in Rick's mailbox. "I've got a response from NamUs. They've given me a number to call." Rick tapped the organization's number into his cell phone and hit speaker. After identifying himself he was transferred to a case worker.

"Detective Starker?" the male voice greeted him. "I'm Tom Chance. You inquired about Howard Heising. His missing person's information came in from an agency in Reno, Nevada. I've got the name and contact information for the detective who submitted the information. Do you have something to write with?"

"I do."

Rick took down the information and thanked the man. He looked up at Patty. "I'll call now if you have time."

"Now's a good time," said Patty.

CHAPTER SIXTEEN

Rick called the number and introduced himself and Patty to a Detective Hayes.

"Why do you think you've found Mr. Heising?" Hayes asked.

Rick explained the double homicide and the method used to make fingerprints. "We ran the prints through AFIS, and they were a match to Heising."

"Those are some awesome prints, and we'll want a copy. This is only the second time I've heard of obtaining prints in that manner."

"It was a first for me," said Rick. "Who reported Heising missing?"

"A woman by the name of Michelle Tang. She claims to be his girlfriend. The two of them lived in Nevada. She said he left the house one day and didn't return. Reported him missing a couple of weeks ago."

"We'll need to talk with her," said Rick. "My partner and I can fly out there."

"I'll let her know that you want to meet and talk with her, and I'll email her contact information to you."

"Thanks," said Rick. After hanging up, he looked at Patty. "Hope it was okay to offer to fly out there."

"Okay with me. And I'm pretty sure I can clear it with the LT. We've got to talk with her. I'll see if he's in his office now."

Patty's cell phone rang. "Let me take this first. It's Becky."

"Hi, Bec."

"Hi, Mom. Got a minute to talk?"

"Sure. What's up?"

"Well, I've given some thought to why I'm so upset about Josh leaving."

"Come up with an answer?" asked Patty.

"I have."

Patty remained silent and could detect a slight sniffle from her daughter.

"I'm afraid I'll lose him, Mom. And I don't want to."

"Becky, I'm proud of you for figuring that out. And I know this is difficult for you."

Becky sniffed. "What if he meets someone? I don't want anyone else but him."

"Becky. Has Josh told you he loves you?"

"All the time."

"And has Josh ever given you reason to believe he's interested in finding someone else?"

"No. Never."

"Well, what makes you think he'll start looking just because he's away at school for a year?"

"I guess I worry that he'll be lonely."

"I'm sure he will at times, Bec. He'll be lonely for you. You'll be able to text and call as often as the two of you are able." Patty laughed. "In fact, you'll probably communicate with each other more during his time in Ireland than you do here."

"I guess that's true. He'll have a lot of new experiences to tell me about."

"The bottom line, Becky, is that you can't control what Josh does when he's not with you. You have to trust him the same way he'll have to trust you."

"What do you mean the same way he'll have to trust me?"

"Well, how do you know he's not worried about you finding someone else?"

"I have no interest in anyone else but Josh. He knows that."

"And he probably figures you know that his interest in girls goes no further than you."

"I hadn't thought about that. I'll call him and ask if we can talk about this. I want to confirm that he'll want to communicate with me as much as I will with him. And I want to assure him that he doesn't need to worry about me becoming interested in anyone else. I love him too much and I could never hurt him."

"Talking with each other is good, Bec. It's always better than guessing. You going back to school now?"

"No, I'm out for the afternoon. I'm going home to work on a paper that's due tomorrow. And to call Josh."

"I'll see you this evening," said Patty.

Seeing that Patty was done with her call, Rick put down his pencil. "I received the contact information we need from NamUs. Heising's girlfriend is expecting to hear from us. Before we call, do you want to confirm with the LT that we can take a trip to Nevada?"

"I'll do that now," Patty said as she got up.

The lieutenant was in his office. "Come in, O'Toole. What's up?"

"We found the girlfriend of our deceased male. She lives in Nevada, and the local PD reported him missing on NamUs a couple of weeks ago. Rick has her contact information, and we'd like to schedule an appointment with her and travel to Nevada for the interview. Is that okay?"

The lieutenant looked down at his desk and then up at Patty. "What do you hope to learn?"

"We hope she can enlighten us on the relationship between the deceased and June Deboe, the Dorisko brothers, someone named Suzie who deals drugs, and a friend of Dorisko who makes beer."

"That's a lot to hope for. Is this not an interview you can take over the phone?"

"We probably could, LT, but you know how much it helps to watch the facial expressions, eye and body movements. Sometimes they tell us as much or more than the spoken words."

"I agree," said the lieutenant. "Let Emma know what times and days you want to travel and where you want to stay. She'll take care of it for you."

"Thanks," Patty said before walking back to her office.

"So we've got the green light to go to Reno," she told Rick. "You want to review the list you've been keeping on where we are thus far on this case?"

"Sure," he said flipping through a few pages in his file. "We have two homicide victims found in a storage unit, whom we've identified as June Deboe and Howard Heising. We suspect drugs were involved due to the kilo found in the storage unit and the fact that June Deboe was dealing drugs."

"Go on," said Patty.

"We know the kilo belonged to David Dorisko, brother of Gerold Dorisko, who rents the storage unit, and we suspect that David knows the woman who was selling to June. We also suspect that he knew one or both of the victims."

Patty tapped the end of her pen on her desk. "We've now identified the girlfriend of our male victim and hope that she can shed some light on why Howard killed June and then was himself murdered. You know, Rick, people caught up in the drug trade are murdered every day. But there's something different about this. I'm not sure how to explain it, but I can feel it in my gut."

"I know what you mean," said Rick. "It's not simply a drug deal gone bad."

Brad stepped into the office, causing both Patty and Rick to look up. "A group of us are getting together to celebrate promotions for Steve and Ted. Want to join us?"

"When?" asked Patty.

Brad looked at his watch. "In about twenty minutes."

"I didn't realize it was so late," Patty said. "Sure, count me in."

Rick hesitated as both Brad and Patty looked to him for a response. "I'll stop by," he said. Brad gave them both a thumbs-up before leaving.

Rick's phone rang and he glanced at caller ID. "It's the girlfriend," he said to Patty before answering. After introducing himself and confirming the name of the caller, he let her know that he was putting her on speaker phone. "We're investigating the death of Howard Heising, and we understand that he was your boyfriend."

"That's right," said Michelle Tang.

"How long had you known Mr. Heising?"

"We've been together for six years."

Rick glanced at Patty and she nodded. "We'd like to meet with you. Your answers to our questions may help us understand why your boyfriend was killed and help find the person who killed him."

"I don't know what I can tell you other than that Howard and I were in love with each other. We have a few friends here, but I don't know what he was doing in Oregon."

A break in her voice as the woman spoke let Patty know that Tang was having a difficult time. "Ms. Tang," Patty said, "we know that this is difficult for you. That's why we'll come to you for our interview. Can we schedule a time and place to meet?"

"Sure. I'm off on Mondays and Tuesdays."

"Give us a minute, Ms. Tang."

Patty and Rick glanced at their calendars. She looked at Rick and asked, "Next Monday at nine?" He agreed. Patty then relayed the information to the caller and the interview was scheduled.

Patty ended the call and looked up at Rick. "I'll ask Emma to schedule our Sunday flight so that we can get into Reno before dark. That means we've got to leave early, so let's meet here at five."

Rick nodded and looked over the schedule.

Patty prepared to leave for the day. "I'll see you at the party."

"See you there," said Rick.

CHAPTER SEVENTEEN

"**S**uzie!"

Suzie looked at her husband standing at the kitchen door. Then to Billy. Tears were running down her son's face and he looked scared. Tom walked over to where Billy was standing and glared at Suzie. "Why are you yelling at him? What's wrong with you?"

She started to walk toward her son with her arms out. "Oh, I'm so sorry, Billy." The boy stepped back.

"Leave him alone," said Tom. "Billy, will you please go play in your room for a while so that your mother and I can talk?" Once Billy had left, Tom stared at his wife with a look of confusion. "What's going on, Suzie? You said you were going to quit smoking and that hasn't happened. You said your problem was your friend Shirley and that you could get yourself under control. You said part of the problem was some guys you'd gone to school with and that you'd ended that relationship. It seems that whether I come home for lunch or at the end of my workday, you greet me while sipping on a glass of wine. So, what is it now, Suzie? You know you've gone too far when your anger is scaring our kids."

Suzie sat down at the kitchen table and began to cry. "Oh, Tommy, I'm so sorry. I really have gone too far. I thought I could just turn off my concern about the people you mentioned but clearly I can't." Suzie sat quietly for a minute as though collecting her thoughts.

"I want to move, Tommy."

"Move?" he said with shock. "Where did that come from?"

"It's because I don't seem to be able to cope with my friends and their problems, and I can see that my stress is taking its toll on you and the kids. Let's move someplace far away, where we'll have a fresh start."

Tom didn't move. He stared at Suzie as her eyeliner began to run and create black lines in the small rivulets of water slowly making their way down her bright red cheeks. He moved his head back and forth as though to communicate a negative response prior to underscoring it with his spoken words. "We're not moving. Our kids have friends here that they've known since starting school. They are good kids from good homes. We're not going to uproot them. I have what I think is a great job. I enjoy my work and make enough money to be able to support my family so that you don't have to work. I'm beginning to think, however, that your getting a job might be the best thing for all of us."

"I just want us to have a fresh start, Tommy. I feel like I'm going crazy here with all the stress I've been under. Can't you at least consider it?"

"Stress you've been under? You have no idea what it requires to go to work every day and perform a job well enough to be promoted into better positions with greater compensation. I've been at this company for ten years, Suzie, and that's exactly what I've done. Do you think I've had days when I'd rather not go to work? Everyone does, but responsible people support their families. You need a job."

"No, Tommy, please. I don't want to have to work. I need to be here when the children come home from school or are on holiday."

"I make enough for us to hire a part-time nanny to fill in until I get home. You have two weeks to find a job, Suzie. I don't care what you do or how much you get paid. I just want you doing something other than sitting at home drinking and screaming at our kids."

"But—"

"Two weeks, Suzie."

"What if I can't find a job?"

"Then you and I will have to have a serious talk about our marriage because I don't want to go on with what it has become."

Both Suzie and Tom were quiet until Tom started to leave. He then turned back to look at Suzie. "You had a part-time job that seemed to pay you well. I never quite understood your periodic bonuses, but you made good money and it got you out of the house. Call whoever it was who hired you then and ask if you can go back to work."

Suzie looked away to the opposite side of the kitchen. "Okay, Tommy. I'll go back to work. You don't need to worry about us. You'll see."

"That's good to hear," Tom said. "Now I suggest you go upstairs and apologize to your son."

"I will, Tommy. I just need a minute to myself."

Once her husband had left the room, Suzie grabbed her phone and sent a text off to Vic. *Need to talk. I'll be there tomorrow at ten.*

* * *

Rick heard the clinking of raised glasses when he walked into the lounge where several of his fellow officers were already making multiple toasts congratulating Steve and Ted on their promotions.

"Can I buy you a drink, Detective?" asked Pete.

For a couple of seconds all Rick could think about was how one drink would taste so good. Just one. What could be the harm? If anyone deserved a drink it was him after all he'd gone through. "Thanks," he said. "I'll have a ginger ale."

Pete laughed. "Right! Now what would you really like?"

"No joke, Pete. I'll have a ginger ale. I've got work to do at home tonight."

"Sure, Detective. I'll be right back with it."

Pete returned with Rick's drink. "Anything new on the double homicide investigation?"

"Nothing that puts us a whole lot closer to some answers."

"I heard there's a complete kit of beer equipment in the storage unit where the murders took place. I'd appreciate your letting me know if that stuff is going to be auctioned off. I'd like to try brewing a few hops myself."

Rick nodded and sipped his drink. "I'll let you know."

Rick looked at his watch, quickly downed the rest of his ginger ale, and went over to the two promoted officers to congratulate them. Steve thanked Rick and then noticed he didn't have a drink in his hand. "What are you drinking?" he asked.

"No, thanks," Rick said. "I've got another stop I've got to make before going home tonight." He left the lounge, got into his car, and headed for the six p.m. AA meeting. Once inside, he sat down toward the back, one seat away from a guy he'd seen many times at the meetings. Sober nineteen years. A real success story. The guy looked across the middle chair and greeted Rick.

"Hi," said Rick.

"Good to see you here," the guy said.

Rick nodded and then looked into the guy's eyes. "Does it ever get easier?"

"Only if you give yourself over to your higher power. Start and end each day with prayer. Thank God for giving you a second chance, and ask for strength to respect each day you're given."

"Thanks," said Rick.

CHAPTER EIGHTEEN

The detectives met at their office at 5:00 a.m. for the two-and-a-half-hour drive from Brookings to the nearest major airport.

"Here's your ticket," said Patty. "If we leave now, we'll have an hour to check in and wait for our plane."

"You sure an hour is enough?"

"It should be. The Medford airport's so small that an hour will give us plenty of time. We'll arrive in Reno about four. That will give us time to rent a car, locate our hotel, and plan tomorrow's interview over dinner."

"I did my part and gassed up my car, anticipating that you'd probably want me to drive."

"You anticipated correctly," said Patty. "Let's hit the road. I don't want to be in a hurry traveling on 199."

"I won't have to hurry," said Rick. "There should be very few drivers on the road at this time of the morning. The only danger will be deer and rocks, and I'll try to avoid both."

Patty and Rick drove south on Highway 101 to 197 where they turned east.

"This is one of the most beautiful parts of this drive," said Patty. "It's always so peaceful meandering through these beautiful giant redwoods."

"I agree," said Rick. "We're fortunate to live in such a scenic area, surrounded by ocean and forest, and I'm sure there's still a lot I don't know about our surroundings. You're always full of interesting facts when we travel any distance. Feel free to educate me as we go along."

"Okay," said Patty. "Since you asked. The first town we'll come to once we turn onto 199 is Hiouchi. The name is American Indian and means 'blue waters.'"

"Well, isn't that a coincidence," said Rick. "I wonder if the owners of Blue Water know that the native name for their restaurant is Hiouchi?"

"Good question to ask next time you eat there," Patty said.

"I know we're still a few miles away, but what can you tell me about Gasquet?"

"Gasquet was named after Horace Gasquet, and he not only founded Gasquet but also Crescent City and Happy Camp."

"The guy must have been one of the wealthiest men around in his time," said Rick.

"I expect probably so," Patty said. "So I'll give you information on one more site we'll see along this highway, in addition to the beautiful Smith River and the redwoods."

"I'm listening," said Rick.

"I'm sure you've noticed the Patrick Creek Lodge just north of Gasquet."

"Can't miss it. Have you been there?"

"I have," said Patty. "You'd like it if historic buildings are of interest. The first lodge on that site was built in the late 1800s. It was called Patrick Creek Stage Station and provided a beautiful resting place for those traveling by stagecoach. Patrick Creek meets the Smith River at that location. There is a campground across the highway and lots of hiking trails. The present lodge was built in 1926 and became a popular stopping place for those traveling along 199. I've eaten there and the food was great. They also have a good-sized bar and a large living room with a huge fireplace. Like so many historic lodges, it's all very cozy."

"Sounds interesting. It would kind of break up the two-hour drive between Highways 5 and 101."

Patty smiled at Rick. "That's the end of your tour. I'm going to review the case file for the duration of our ride."

"Thanks," said Rick. "Your knowledge of little-known facts is one of the reasons I like traveling with you."

"Really?" asked Patty. "What's another reason?"

"Huh?"

"You said that my tour-guide knowledge is one of the reasons you like traveling with me. What's one of the other reasons?"

Rick thought for a moment and smiled. "You let me drive."

The rest of the drive was uneventful, and Rick pulled into the airport parking lot right on time. The detectives walked up to the ticket counter and showed their identification.

"Our firearms are in locked cases within the luggage we're checking," said Patty.

The airline rep thanked the detectives, attached an additional information card to the suitcases and set them on the carousel. They progressed through security and found seats at the gate.

"Did you see what was holding up the security line in front of us?" Patty asked Rick. "I was beginning to wonder if I'd made a mistake thinking we only needed to get here an hour early."

"I did notice. It was a disagreement between a passenger and the TSA agent. Were you able to hear the conversation between the two?"

"No," said Patty. "I just noticed that the TSA woman seemed to be holding back a smile while she tried to get information out of an older woman. You were in front of me. Could you see or hear anything?"

"I could and I heard."

Patty waited for Rick to go on. "So what was the hold-up?"

"The passenger had a bottle of liquid in her carry-on that exceeded the three-ounce limit. She evidently figured that it shouldn't be a problem because of the contents and was explaining to the TSA woman that she, the passenger, would need the bottle that evening."

"What did the TSA woman do?"

Rick smiled. "She held up the bottle high enough for the other TSA personnel to see it and loudly asked if there was an exception to the rule for a large bottle of personal lubricant?"

Patty laughed. "Oh, my gosh. What did the passenger do?"

"The first thing she did was to quit protesting. Then she quickly told the TSA woman to throw the bottle away and get her through the line."

"That's hilarious," said Patty. "And, now that I think of it, that scene should have been filmed and used on TV for the product ad. That woman had to be at least seventy."

Rick laughed. "Guess it works."

* * *

Patty and Rick met Michelle Tang at her home. They had discussed their interview process on the flight.

"Since you found Michelle through NamUs," Patty said, "why don't you lead the questioning?"

Rick took on a look of surprise, opening his eyes wide and then expressing his shock with a "Wow! You're really going to let me lead? To what do I owe this great favor?"

Patty rolled her eyes. "You keep that up and I'll take back my decision."

Rick smiled. "Okay. I'll start, but you jump in anytime."

Michelle was home and expecting the detectives when they arrived. She led them into her living room where Patty sat on the couch and Rick in a La-Z-Boy.

"Thank you for meeting with us," Rick said.

"Sure. I'd like to know what Howard was doing in Oregon, and why he was killed."

"Had he been to Oregon before?" asked Rick.

"Not while we were together."

"Did Howard smoke pot or use drugs?"

"Never," said Michelle. "Just the opposite. He volunteered for one of the local organizations that helps young people to stay clear of drugs."

"What kind of work did he do?"

"He was an electrician but was laid off a few months ago. The owners of the small company he worked for retired and closed the business. He'd been looking for work. That could be why he went to Oregon. Maybe he didn't want to tell me that he might find a job there until he could say for sure that he was employed."

"What about you?" asked Rick. "Smoke pot or use drugs?"

"I work for a day care center. I enjoy my work, and good jobs are hard to come by nowadays with unemployment being so low. I would be canned quickly if I showed up at work smelling like pot or high on drugs. Besides, I don't need that stuff. Howard and I had a good life."

"Did the two of you hang out with friends here?"

"Sure, we have a few friends. Why?"

"I'm just wondering if any of them have also gone missing?"

"Oh, I don't think so or I'd have heard about it."

"Any of them smoke pot or use drugs?" Rick asked.

"The ones I'm close to don't have anything to do with drugs. I don't know what the others do at home, but they don't use when they're around me and Howard." Michelle's eyes teared, mentioning Howard's name. "I don't want to talk about him in the past. I want him back here with me." Patty moved a box of tissues that were in the middle of the table. Michelle pulled a few out of the box and proceeded to dry the tears on her face and blow her nose.

"Michelle, it's very important that you think about this next question before you answer. Did Howard own a gun?"

"Yes. He believed in self-protection and always kept a gun in our home."

"Is the gun here now?"

"I'm sure it is. Do you want me to get it?"

Patty stood up. "Do you mind if I go with you?"

"No," said the young woman.

Before they walked out of the room, Rick asked where the bathroom was.

"Off the hall next to the front door."

Patty and Michelle walked into the master bedroom. Patty took the opportunity to look around. Michelle reached onto a shelf in the closet and pulled down a carved wooden box. "Howard kept his gun in here when he was home." Michelle opened the box and found it empty.

"When was the last time you saw Howard's gun in that box?" Patty asked.

"Oh, maybe a couple of months ago. Not long before he disappeared."

"Would he have taken it on a trip to Oregon?"

"Yes, now that you mention it. He probably would have hidden it in the car for protection."

"Do you know what kind of gun it was?"

"Well, I don't know much about guns, but he called it a 1911."

"Okay," Patty said. "Let's go back into the living room."

Patty glanced at Rick as she passed him to sit on the couch. He moved his head from side to side.

"Michelle," Rick said, "is there anything at all that you can tell us about Howard, his friends, or his plans that might help us to better understand why he went to Oregon?"

She leaned her head down. "I didn't want to mention this."

"Mention what?"

"I know that Howard loves me, but I did hear him on the phone a few days before he left. He was talking with a woman. I didn't understand what it was they were talking about, but he kept saying 'Okay.'"

"How do you know it was a woman?" Rick asked.

"He called her Suzie."

"Did he mention Suzie's last name?"

"No. Just Suzie. I think she must have been asking him to do something he didn't want to do. At first, he said he wouldn't do what she asked. Then, before hanging up, he said okay."

"What was his mood when he was talking with this Suzie?" Patty asked.

"He sounded mad and frustrated. I mentioned it to him the last night before he disappeared. I asked who Suzie was."

"What did he say?" asked Patty.

"He said she was just some old friend. Someone he'd known years ago while going to college. He assured me there was nothing for me to worry about."

"You mentioned Howard had been out of work for a while. How have you been able to pay your rent and monthly food and utility bills?"

"Well, I make enough to cover some of it, and he was receiving unemployment. He also told me that he'd been saving some of his paycheck."

"Do you know where Howard went to college and possibly met this Suzie?"

"I think so. He went to a couple of colleges in California. One was in Oakland and the other was in Eureka. He didn't talk much about those days, though. I got the impression he wasn't happy."

Patty stood up to let Rick know she was done, and she gave one of her cards to Michelle. "That's all the questions we have for now. We'll let you know if anything else comes up. You're welcome to contact us anytime, and we'd like for you to call if you think of anything that might help us out."

"Okay," said Michelle. "I hope you find out who killed him. He didn't deserve to die."

Patty and Rick left and drove back to the airport where they turned in their rental car and boarded a plane to Medford.

"We've got to find this Suzie," said Rick. "She seems to be the common denominator among all of the parties to our homicide."

Patty nodded. "I can't put my finger on it, but there's something bothering me about Howard having known Suzie in college. What were they doing fifteen years ago at college that would negatively affect their lives today?"

"You think they were having an affair?" asked Rick

"I don't know, Rick. I get the feeling it's more than that. Michelle seemed pretty grounded in the idea that she and Howard had a successful relationship."

"Yeah," said Rick, "but even people in good relationships sometimes get lured into having affairs."

"Would he walk off and leave Michelle, and travel all the way to the Oregon coast for an affair with someone he knew in college during a time when, according to Michelle, he was unhappy?"

"That's a good question, Patty."

"What if he was being blackmailed?" asked Patty.

"About what?"

"I don't know yet. Maybe he did drugs in college, and Suzie threatened to tell Michelle."

"No, I don't see it," said Rick. "That was fifteen years ago, and I didn't find drugs in her bathroom cabinet while we were there. If he's been with her for six years and hasn't smoked or used anything, I don't think it would matter to her what he did fifteen years ago."

"Yeah, I guess you're right."

CHAPTER NINETEEN

Suzie walked into Vic's lounge and up to the bar, where she sat and waited as Vic filled drink orders for a couple seated at the end of the bar.

"How about those Ducks!" the man exclaimed. "They're one heck of a team."

"They're doing great," said Vic. "Making us all proud the way they've played this year."

"Sweetheart," said the woman with the Ducks fan, "you promised you wouldn't talk sports."

"Oh, honey. Okay." The guy gave a wink to Vic and turned his attention to his date.

Vic walked over to Suzie. "What's your problem?"

"I'm leaving."

Vic put down the bar towel he'd been holding and put both palms on the bar. "What do you mean, you're leaving?"

"I've got to get away from here, Vic."

"Have you told Tom?"

"He doesn't want to move. Says he won't move the kids."

"Then why are you telling me you're going to leave? Tom doesn't want to move."

Suzie exhaled loudly and looked down at the bar. "I'm leaving without him."

Vic took a step back. He looked to see if there were empty glasses on the bar and then looked back at Suzie. "You're nuts. Do you know that? You can't leave Tom. How will you live?"

"I'll get a job."

"Get a job?" Vic asked, loud enough that the couple stopped talking and looked over at him and Suzie. He waved at the couple, letting them know everything was okay, and then turned back to Suzie. "The only job you've ever had that paid more than minimum wage was selling drugs, and you've never had to worry about supporting yourself. Now you're telling me that you're going to leave your four-bedroom home in the suburbs, your fancy car and clothes, and a husband who supports you and your kids. All so that you can become a full-time dealer?"

Suzie began to cry. "I've got to, Vic. I had a phone call from someone who said Dorisko asked him to call. He said the police were asking questions about me. They know who I am. I can't go back to jail."

Vic shook his head and looked over again at the couple. He walked to the end of the bar. "Two of the same?"

"Yeah," said the guy. "Sounds like you've got girlfriend trouble."

Vic looked at Suzie. "Just a friend," he said. He fixed up the couple with fresh drinks, filled an order for one of the barmaids, and came back to Suzie.

"Look, Suzie. I got a call from the same guy. Dorisko's just trying to scare you. He thinks you're going to crack. If the cops knew who you were, they'd have been to your house by now."

"You think?" asked Suzie.

"Yeah. He's messing with you. And if you don't get a grip on yourself, you'll lose Tom and your kids. Now go home and let me work."

Suzie stepped down from the bar stool. "I can't go to prison. I'll leave Tom and the kids before I get stuck in there."

"Quit worrying about it and go home."

"Vic?"

"What?"

"Maybe we should tell the police about the drugs. We can blame it on Dorisko. Maybe we'll get a reduced sentence if we turn in Dorisko."

Vic looked at Suzie and shook his head. "You're tired, Suzie. Go home and quit worrying. We all need to continue to remain calm."

"Okay, Vic. Maybe you're right. See ya."

Suzie left the bar. Vic served another round to the couple at the end of the bar and noticed it was getting busier as he filled a couple more orders for the young barmaid.

"Everything okay?" she asked him.

Vic winked at her. "Always, honey, when you're here."

The barmaid smiled and walked off to her customers. Vic looked at the past calls on his phone, found what he wanted and hit dial. A low voice was heard at the other end of the line.

"Yeah?"

"My name's Vic. You called me a few days ago. Gave me a message from Dorisko."

"Yeah?"

"I need to get a message back to him. Tell him that his concerns about Suzie are spot on. Tell him I'm concerned too. Ask if he knows anyone who can take care of the problem."

"You want me to ask Dorisko if he knows anyone who can take care of your problem?"

"Not just my problem," Vic said. "She's Dorisko's problem too. Just get that message to him."

"I think you've got me mixed up with Dorisko's errand boy," said the voice. "I just happened to be getting out when he passed that earlier message on to me. I've got no plans to go back in."

"Don't you know some way of getting the message to him?"

"What is it you really want taken care of, man?"

Vic hesitated to say any more to someone he didn't know. But he was beginning to feel a little paranoid about Suzie. "I need help from someone who knows how to quiet a woman who's beginning to talk too much."

"This sounds serious," said the voice. "How quiet do you want this woman?"

"I don't want to hear from her again," said Vic.

There was an eerie silence on the phone. Like in a chess game where each player is thinking ahead before making a move.

"Let's say I know someone who can help. What's it worth to you?"

Vic knew this question was coming, and he'd thought about how much he could spend without putting his bar in jeopardy. "Two thousand," he said.

The man at the other end of the line laughed. It was a thick, low, gravelly laugh, and it worried Vic, thinking about the kind of guy he was dealing with.

Vic coughed. "Seems I've made a mistake. I didn't want to have to mortgage my business for this. Forget I mentioned it," he said and ended the call.

Two minutes later Vic's phone rang.

"Five thousand," said the voice. "Two now and three when the job's done."

"Four thousand," Vic said. "One now. A second when the job's finished, and two more when I read her obituary."

Vic thought he could hear a low growl on the line. "Send photos, contact information, and the initial grand to the following address." Vic took down the information and looked up to find the barmaid waiting for him to fill her order.

* * *

Patty and Rick were at the office early the next morning. Rick had brought a white bakery bag to work and offered Patty an old-fashioned chocolate-covered doughnut. She'd filled their mugs with coffee in the kitchen and handed Rick's to him.

"June and Howard's murders are becoming more complicated every day," she said. "If Howard wasn't a drug user, what was he doing with June, and why would he kill her? And why did the guy who owns the beer equipment back off? What's he worried about? Do you think he knows Suzie? David Dorisko says he had nothing to do with the murders and yet he won't talk to us about Suzie or the brewer. Why?"

Rick took a sip of his coffee and set his mug on the napkin with his signature pastry. "Let's go over what we know. June may have had a connection with Howard because both June and Howard knew Suzie. I think David was also connected to Howard and is connected to Suzie judging from the expression on his face when we asked if he knew her. Maybe we need to check with the colleges Howard attended and see if we can confirm a relationship at that time between Suzie, Howard, David, and the brewer."

"You want Oakland or Eureka?" asked Patty.

"I'll take Eureka."

Patty googled Oakland colleges. "Looks like the junior college we want in Oakland is Laney. Maybe the current Admissions person was there fifteen years ago, and Howard did something to make an impression."

"Maybe," said Rick. "We should also ask about Suzie and Dorisko while we're at it."

Patty nodded and called Laney College Admissions while Rick called College of the Redwoods. The woman assisting Patty seemed eager to help.

"We did have a David Dorisko here during the time frame you requested. He was only here for two semesters. Looks like he was asked to leave."

"You mean he was expelled?" Patty asked.

"All it says is that the dean asked him to leave due to drug use."

"Can you look for a Howard Heising?"

The assistant continued to read the computer files. "Yes, Howard was here at the same time."

"How long?" asked Patty.

"He also left after one year, however there are no file notes as to why he left."

"Is there mention of drugs?" asked Patty.

"No. No mention of anything relating to him or his leaving."

"I'd like whatever information you have on them during the time they were students."

"Okay. I'll email it to you."

"Thanks," said Patty. "Is there any way that you can find someone by first name only?"

"I can try, but a common name may come up with multiple listings."

"I can work with that. The name is Suzie. I don't know if it's a nickname for Susan, Susana, or Suzanne."

Patty waited while the woman input each name. "There were two Susans here during the same time that Heising and Dorisko attended."

"Great. I'll need their contact information too. Did either leave school after two semesters?"

"Let me see," she said.

Patty could hear tapping on computer keys.

"Yes. Susan Browne was here a year and left when the others did. There is a note in her file indicating that she too was using drugs."

"Were you working at the college back then?"

She laughed before answering. "Oh, yes. I've been at this desk for twenty years, and some days it feels like twice that long."

"Is there anything you can remember that went on at the college during the year that Heising, Dorisko, and Browne were there?"

"What do you mean?"

"Well," said Patty, "an incident of some kind that would have involved those three students?"

"Nothing I can remember right now. But if it's important, I can talk with a couple of my co-workers who've been here as long as I have. I'll call you if they remember something."

"That would be helpful," said Patty. "Thank you."

Rick was finishing up a call when Patty ended hers with the college. She googled Susan Browne and about fifteen names came up, along with half a dozen photographs of different people.

When Rick ended his call, Patty let him know what she'd learned. "I'm hoping one of these Susan Brownes is our Suzie. I'll call Eugene PD and ask for help."

"She's probably tried hard," said Rick, "to stay off the radar of the local police. But we only need one contact for access to her married name."

Patty looked at her directory of investigators in other agencies and found the name of Detective Strand. She called the Eugene Police Department, was transferred to Strand's office, and explained why she was calling. "We're investigating a double homicide that may involve drugs. We have a name and hope you can tell us whether there have been any contacts with this woman."

"I'll do what I can," said Strand. "What's the name?"

"Susan Browne," said Patty. "Browne is her maiden name, and she goes by Suzie."

"Give me a minute," he said as he input Susan Browne into his computer program search engine. "I don't come up with a Susan Browne."

Patty let out an immediate sigh. "Well, it was a long shot, but thanks."

Strand quickly responded, "I said I have no Susan Browne. Not that I didn't have anything. I'm looking through a list of names that are close to Susan Browne, and there is a Susan Browne Mantis."

Patty repeated the name out loud so that Rick could hear. He smiled and nodded.

"That could be her, Detective," Patty said. "I'm going to put you on speaker phone so that my partner can hear what you've got. Any contacts?"

"We don't show any citations, but there are a couple of contacts."

Rick raised his eyebrows. "Crimes against her?"

"Yes. We had an accident downtown a couple of years ago. A drunk driver rammed into a BMW parked along the side of the road. The BMW belonged to Susan B. Mantis. More recently, Susan B. Mantis was involved in credit card fraud."

"I'm surprised she'd report it," said Rick.

"She didn't," said the detective. "Nordstrom's called us to report the stolen card while the responsible was trying to use it. We contacted Mantis to let her know. You think she's your suspect?"

"There's a good chance," said Patty. "She's the right age, and witnesses have mentioned her driving a nice car. Even if it's not the same car she drives now, it shows that she can afford luxury. Does your information mention her having kids?"

"Let me look at the report," said Strand. "It doesn't mention kids, but there was a car seat in the BMW."

"We need to bring her in," said Patty. "If it is the same woman, she's been dealing drugs for years and therefore could be armed. Detective Starker and I can arrive tomorrow at about one. Would you be able to keep her home under surveillance until we get there? Follow her or her husband if one of them leaves the house?"

"I can arrange that," said Strand.

"Thanks, Detective." Said Patty. 'We'll meet up with you at the PD to coordinate a plan with you and your officers."

CHAPTER TWENTY

Patty and Rick left early for Eugene, giving themselves a little extra time in the event of roadwork on the highway. At twelve forty-five they pulled into the Eugene Police Department.

"This could be a big step toward wrapping up our investigation," Rick said. "At least, we'll have the elusive Suzie. She seems to be the link to everyone involved."

"She does," said Patty. "I hope she's at home without her kids. They don't need to see this."

Patty and Rick met with Strand. "Thanks for your surveillance."

"Sure. We've had someone watching the house from five p.m. yesterday. One of our officers is still there. No one has seen a woman enter or leave the home. A man we assume is her husband left the house with two young children this morning about seven. One of our officers followed him. He dropped the kids off at school and then went on to an office building downtown. He's still there. So the woman is either alone at home, or she did not come home yesterday."

Patty nodded. "Rick and I will approach the house from the front. Can you watch the back?" she asked Strand.

"Sure. I'll have another officer in front ready to follow you in if necessary."

"Let's go," said Patty. "If we find she's not home, Rick and I will go to the husband's place of business and talk with him. I'd appreciate your keeping an officer on the house in the event the suspect arrives after we've left."

Once everyone was in place, the detectives approached the front door and Patty knocked. "Police!" She knocked again and rang the doorbell. When no one responded, she spoke into her portable radio. "No answer in the front. Is the back locked up?"

Strand responded. "Yeah. Locked up tight. No response to my knock on the door."

"Rick and I will head downtown and talk with the husband. Let us know if the suspect arrives back home."

"Will do. Let me know what you learn from the husband."

Rick and Patty drove to an older four-story building in the downtown area. They parked on the street, entered a common lobby, and found the names of five businesses on the directory.

"Let's start on the second floor," said Patty. "We'll work our way up from there."

The elevator opened on the second floor across from a directional sign with two business names. Rick went down the hall to the left and Patty to the right. She opened the door and walked into the reception room for Easy Clean Flooring.

"May I help you?" asked the young woman sitting at the desk.

"I hope so," said Patty. "I'm here to meet with a Mr. Mantis and I can't remember what company he works for. Am I in the right place?"

"No, but I can help. Everyone in the building knows Mr. Mantis. He works upstairs for Pie In The Sky Inventions on the third floor. They're the only ones on that floor."

"Thank you," said Patty before stepping back out of the office. She met Rick at the elevator. The detectives looked at each other and said simultaneously, "Third floor."

Pie In The Sky had a glass entry door across the hall from the elevator. A middle-aged male receptionist greeted them as they walked in.

"May I help you?" he asked.

"We're here to see Mr. Mantis," said Patty.

"I'll be happy to call Mr. Mantis for you. Who may I tell him is here?"

Patty showed the receptionist her police ID. "Detectives O'Toole and Starker."

"I'll let him know. Please have a seat."

Patty and Rick remained standing. Within a minute or two, a middle-aged man walked into the reception area. "I'm Thomas Mantis."

"I'm Detective O'Toole and this is Detective Starker, with the Brookings Police Department."

"Police?" he replied. "What can I do for you?"

"Is there a place we can talk privately?" Patty asked.

"Yes, of course. My office is just down the hall."

The detectives sat down across the desk from Mantis. Patty noticed an eight-by-eleven photograph of Mantis, two children, and an attractive woman with shoulder-length blond hair.

"Is this your family?" she asked, pointing toward the photo.

Mantis looked at the photo and stroked his furrowed brow. "Yes, it is."

"Is your wife's name Suzie?" asked Patty.

"It is," he replied. "Has something happened to Suzie?"

"We don't know. We're investigating a crime, and we have reason to believe your wife may be tied to our investigation."

"What kind of crime?"

"Drug dealing," said Patty.

Mantis slouched back in his chair. "Drugs? But Suzie's never used drugs. And we have two children."

Patty could see the man's facial expression change as he spoke, from one of panic to disbelief, and now to fear.

"Do you have proof of her involvement?" he asked.

"We have witnesses who will be able to confirm whether your wife is the Suzie we're looking for. If it is her, she could be in danger. We need to talk with her as soon as possible. Do you know where she is?"

Mantis appeared to be deep in thought as he stared at the top of his desk. Patty wasn't sure he'd heard her. "Mr. Mantis," she repeated. "Do you know where your wife is?"

"She didn't come home yesterday," he said. "I don't know where she is."

Rick leaned forward to get the attention of Mantis. "Have you tried texting or calling her?"

Mantis looked up at Rick. His blue eyes now filled with tears. "I've been texting all morning and she hasn't responded. I've left three voice mail messages. She lied to me, didn't she? All this time she's been lying to me."

"Lying to you about what?" Rick asked.

"About the guy she was texting. She said he was an old high school friend. I believed her. But lately she's become nervous and irritable. I knew there was a problem, but I guess I just couldn't admit to myself that she'd cheat on me."

"Who's the guy she's been texting?" Patty asked. "What's his name?"

"All I know is Vic."

"Vic," Patty said. "That helps. Do you know where Vic lives or works?"

"No. At least, not exactly. I know he's someplace here in Eugene." Mantis suddenly took on a frantic look. "My children!"

"Where are they now?" Patty asked.

"I dropped them off at school. They'll need to be picked up soon."

"Call the school now," said Patty. "Be clear that only you should be allowed to take the children from school. Give my name and phone number to the principal if confirmation is needed. Do you understand?"

Mantis nodded and looked up the school phone number on his phone.

The detectives stood up to leave. "Call me immediately if you hear from your wife," said Patty. "Tell her she needs to turn herself in. Tell her she's in danger."

Mantis nodded again as he tapped *call* and connected with the school.

Patty and Rick left and began driving back to the PD.

"Do you believe him?" asked Patty.

"I do," said Rick. "He was genuinely shocked when we told him why we were there. It must seem unreal to learn that your spouse and the mother of your children has been dealing drugs and may have a secret lover."

"It's more than unreal, Rick," said Patty. "It can be a nightmare. Though my ex wasn't into drugs, he kept his affair hidden until a couple days before leaving Becky and me, and taking off with his new love. I was devastated, and it took counselling and talking with other women who'd had similar experiences for me to get back some semblance of self-respect." Before Patty could go on, her cell phone rang. "O'Toole."

"O'Toole, this is Strand. We've just responded to a 911 call. Hit-and-run. I'm at Riverbend Hospital where the victim was brought. Her name is Suzie Mantis."

"We're on our way," said Patty.

Upon their arrival, Strand updated Patty and Rick on Suzie's condition. "She's in ICU and in a coma. The doctors are not sure if she'll make it. Were you able to talk with the husband?"

"We did," said Patty. "He says Suzie's been texting some guy named Vic. He confronted her about the texts, and she lied. He said she's been nervous and agitated lately. Have you notified him that his wife is here?"

"My officer called, and Mr. Mantis is on his way."

"Did she have a cell phone with her when she was brought in?"

"She did," said Strand "It's in her purse."

"How fast can you get a search warrant?" asked Patty.

"Give me an hour."

"We need the warrant to cover her personal belongings, car, house, and anything else you can think of. We might get lucky and find contact information on the phone for this guy, Vic, that the husband mentioned."

"I'll call you when it comes through," said Strand. "It may also have evidence for our hit-and-run. You can wait at the PD if you want. There's hot coffee."

"Sounds good. Is there an empty office we can use?"

"Should be an empty interview room," said Strand.

"Before we leave, I'd like to make a suggestion," said Rick. "If Suzie Mantis is part of a drug ring that could have ties to a double homicide, there are a lot of bad people out there who do not want her to survive. It was probably one of them who caused the wreck with the intent to kill her. The media are going to be showing up here soon for a statement. We can let the public know that she's in a coma, but let's not tell them if she wakes up. That way we can get information we'll need from her, and possibly keep her safe."

"Good idea," Patty said. "Okay with you, Strand?"

"Sure. I like it. I'll keep an officer outside her room twenty-four seven. What about her husband and children?"

"I suggest he be told to take his kids to a relative's house. Somewhere safe. He should also think of leaving until we've arrested the responsible."

"I'll talk with him," said Strand.

"We need to go back to Brookings for a couple of days," said Patty. "We'll leave in the morning."

Patty and Rick drove back to the Eugene PD and waited in the break room for the warrant to come through. When it did, an officer brought Suzie's phone to Patty along with a pen and Chain of Evidence log. He led them down the hall to a room with a desk and a couple of chairs.

"An hour and fifteen minutes," said Patty. "That must be some kind of a record for obtaining a warrant."

"Yep. Guess it pays to have an uncle who's a judge," said Rick.

* * *

Vic was drying glasses he'd washed and setting them on a shelf behind the bar.

The mesmerizing sound of Linda Ronstadt's *Blue Bayou* seemed to waft from one table to the next. He looked around at the glassy-eyed patrons who were unwinding before facing whomever they would or would not find at home. Vic felt a sudden deep appreciation for his girlfriend Lorin. The melancholy moment was interrupted by the sound of his cell phone indicating he had a call. Vic picked up.

"It's done," said the voice. "I want another grand deposited into my account before five p.m."

Vic heard the call end. He looked around the room again and then at the bar towel in his hand. He found a wet spot and began rubbing his towel over the bar.

CHAPTER TWENTY-ONE

Patty was stroking her thumb against the phone. "There must be a thousand texts here, and so far I've only seen a few between Suzie and a Vic. There's nothing that identifies his location."

"You've only been looking for fifteen minutes," said Rick. "Let's go back as far as we can. Give the phone to me when you need a break."

"Wait a minute. I may have spoken too soon," said Patty. "Vic tells Suzie to call him now because his barmaid has just arrived."

"That's good," said Rick. "He could work at a restaurant or bar here in Eugene. You keep going through the text messages, and I'll make a few calls."

"Oh, my gosh!" said Patty.

"What?" asked Rick.

"Here are a couple of messages between Suzie and June. Suzie's text tells June to meet the next day in the college parking lot. She tells June to bring the cash. That confirms the connection between those two."

Rick smiled. "We've got her for the drugs. And she probably knows the other players."

"We're getting close to something big, Rick. You make the calls and see if there's a Vic tending bar out there. I'm going to call the LT and let him know what we've got."

Forty-five minutes later, Rick had made a half-dozen calls to restaurants and bars in Eugene. None had a bartender named Vic. He hit pay-dirt with the seventh call.

A man answered with the name of the lounge. "Bayou Lounge."

"Is this Vic?" asked Rick.

"Yeah. Who's this?"

"This is Detective Starker. I need to talk with you about Suzie Mantis."

Rick listened to the silence at the other end of the line. "Hello? You still there?"

"Yeah, I'm here. Is she supposed to be one of my patrons?"

"From what I understand, she's more to you than a patron."

More silence.

"Okay. She and I know each other. Is there something wrong with her?"

"Interesting you should ask," said Rick. "I need to talk with you about Suzie. Stay put. My partner and I will be there in fifteen minutes."

Vic nervously looked through his phone at the text messaging he and Suzie had shared while his barmaid stood patiently waiting for her order. "Something wrong, Vic?"

"Nothing I can't handle," he said. "Lorin will be here any minute, and I've got something else I'll have to deal with first. Can you show her to a table when she comes in, and let her know I won't be long?"

"Sure thing, Vic. Can you fill my tray first?"

Twelve minutes later, the detectives walked into his lounge. Looking around, they recognized two of the patrons: one for a DUII and another for sexual assault. Rick noticed a young woman who had walked in just ahead of him and Patty. She was directed by the barmaid to one of the tables. The woman caught Rick's eye and turned away. The barmaid looked up at the man tending bar and nodded her head toward Patty and Rick. He saw the detectives, set a couple of empty glasses in the sink, picked up a towel and began wiping down the bar.

"Are you Vic?" Patty asked.

"Yeah."

"Vic who?" ask Rick.

"Thompson."

Patty knew the bartender wouldn't ask for identification. Wouldn't want to alarm his patrons.

"How well do you know Suzie Mantis?" Patty asked.

"Not real well. She and I have known each other for a while."

Patty looked at Rick, and he leaned forward placing his hands on the bar. "We've read your text messages, Vic. We know your relationship with Suzie is more than casual. We also know that the two of you are acquainted with David Dorisko."

Vic paled.

"We can do this here or down at the station," said Rick.

Vic looked to Rick and then Patty. "What do you want to know?"

"When was the last time you saw Suzie Mantis?" Patty asked.

"She was here last week," said Vic.

"Why'd she come in?"

Vic rubbed his towel across the bar. "She was worried about her marriage. Worried that her husband would learn she was having an affair."

"The way we hear it," Patty said, "Suzie's affair has been with you."

"Well, you heard wrong. She's nothing but trouble."

"But she comes to you with her marriage problems?" asked Rick.

"I told her to go home and leave me out of it."

Patty pulled a photo of June Deboe out of a plastic sleeve and set it down on the bar in front of Vic. "Do you know her?"

Vic looked at the photo, paused, and then responded, "No."

"You sure?" Patty picked up the photo and extended her arm. "Look again."

He took the photo from her with one hand and looked again. "Don't know her." Vic looked around the room and then at the detectives. "Why are you asking me about Suzie? Is she in trouble?"

"She's in the hospital," Patty said.

Vic stood silent, his eyebrows furrowed as though confused. "Hospital? What's she doing there?"

"She was in an accident," said Patty.

Vic was visibly shaken. "And she survived?"

"She's in a coma."

Patty glanced at Rick. He nodded and picked up the questions. "How do you know Dorisko?"

"Dorisko?" asked Vic.

"Yeah. David Dorisko. He seems to know you."

Vic looked at the floor and moved his head side to side. "I used to use. Dorisko supplied me with what I needed. I've been clean for three years now and want nothing to do with him."

The barmaid stepped up to the bar, set her empties aside, and waited to give her order to Vic.

"Look," Vic said, "I've got a business to run and you've got nothing on me. So I'm asking you both to get out of my bar."

Patty and Rick glanced at each other. "Just one more question," Patty said. "Do you brew beer?"

Vic paused before speaking. "No time for anything like that. Now leave."

"We will for now," Patty said, "but we'll be back with more questions."

The detectives walked out of the bar and drove back to the PD.

"He seemed genuinely surprised," said Rick, "when you mentioned Suzie's in the hospital."

"I saw that too. So, do you think he was surprised to learn she's in the hospital or that she's alive?"

"That's the million-dollar question."

Patty nodded. "Up until now the only thing we've really had on Vic is associated with the beer equipment and coke. And we'll know for sure whether the equipment is his when the prints we just got are taken off the photo of June. But, after our little chat, I'd say he's a suspect in the hit-and-run and may be involved in the murder of Heising. I'll let Detective Strand know of Vic's affiliation with Suzie. Strand will want to look at him for the accident."

* * *

Lorin had a quizzical look on her face as Vic pondered what he would tell her. How much should he tell her? What can he do about the two thousand he gave to a guy he refers to as 'The Voice' when he now knows Suzie didn't die in the car crash? What if Suzie comes out of her coma and starts talking? Who else, besides The Voice, knows that he paid to have Suzie killed? Did The Voice tell Dorisko?

Lorin left her table against the wall, walked up to the bar and sat down. She set her purse on the seat next to her.

"Hi, sweetie," Vic said with a smile. "I didn't mean to ignore you, but I had some unfinished business to take care of."

"Unfinished business?" asked Lorin. "I thought this was your only business."

"Well, it is. Those two people are interested in buying a bar and were asking if I would consider selling to them." Vic looked toward the end of the bar and saw that he needed two more draft beers. He began drawing them when Lorin asked, "And?"

Vic set the beers down. "And what?"

"You seem to have your mind someplace else, Vic." She picked up her purse. "I'm going home. Let me know when you're ready to give me your attention."

Vic quickly grabbed Lorin's arm as she turned around. "Please don't go, Lorin. I'm sorry for being such a jerk. I've just got a lot on my mind is all."

Lorin turned back and faced Vic. "It helps to talk out your problems." She glanced toward the guy waiting for his beer. "Take care of your customers and then talk to me. Tell me what's bothering you."

Vic hesitated and Lorin pulled away. "Okay," he said. "Maybe you're right. Give me a few minutes and then we can talk."

Vic took care of three customers at the bar and a tray for the barmaid. When he turned his attention back to Lorin, she was watching news on the TV above the bar. "Tragic accident," she said. "A woman is in a coma because someone crashed into her car and then drove off. Did you hear about this?"

Vic looked up at the TV screen and saw Suzie's smashed car. The BMW had been hit on the driver's side. He was surprised that The Voice was able to drive away, considering the damage to the BMW. "No, I hadn't heard."

Lorin shook her head. "I hope they catch whoever did that to her. Someone needs to go to prison for a very long time. Don't you agree, Vic?"

"Yeah. A long time."

Lorin looked up at Vic. He caught her eyes and then looked away.

"So," she said, "let's talk. Tell me what's bothering you."

Vic looked at Lorin. "Those weren't prospective buyers for my bar. They were detectives."

Lorin's eyes grew large. "Detectives! What were they talking to you about?"

"They think I might know something about some cocaine that was found in a storage shed."

"Cocaine? Why would the police think you know anything about drugs?"

Vic hung his head. "I used to know some people in college who used drugs. That woman who's now in a coma is one of them. She contacts me now and then and recently sent me a couple of text messages. The detectives saw my texts and thought I might know something about her accident."

"Wait a minute, Vic. You just told me you didn't know about the woman on the news. Now you tell me that she's an old friend who you've been texting?"

"I didn't see the woman's face on the news, so I wasn't sure it was her. And don't read anything into our texting. There's nothing going on between us."

"Well," said Lorin, "I'm still confused. What does your knowing her have to do with the drugs found in a storage shed?"

Vic was silent a minute as he thought about Lorin's question. "Well, I know the brother of the owner of the storage shed, and he's in jail for possessing the cocaine. He also knows this woman who's now in a coma."

Lorin squirmed a bit on her bar stool. "This isn't making any sense to me, Vic. You're telling me that the police know who owns the cocaine and that they have the owner in jail. So why would they show up here to talk with you? There must be something you're not telling me."

Vic looked down the bar and saw that a couple had just sat down. "Give me a minute," he said to Lorin. He filled the drink order and returned to see his girlfriend staring at him.

"Look, babe. It's just a complicated misunderstanding right now. So I'm asking you to trust me that it's all going to be okay. It's not important. What's important is that I love you, and I really need to know that you love me too."

The barmaid stepped up to the bar with an empty tray and a new drink order. Vic looked at Lorin, who was now sitting quietly while he talked and worked.

"I've got to get back to work," he said. "I tell you what. Let's plan a vacation. We can talk about it when I get home. You think about where you want to go. Would you like that?"

"I don't know, Vic. I'm awfully confused right now. I'm thinking maybe it would be good for us to split up for a while."

"Split up?"

Lorin stood up, picked up her purse, and walked out of the bar.

Vic nervously walked back and forth along the inside of the bar. He straightened a few wine glasses on one of many glass shelves and noticed how the blue lights he'd installed years ago reflected off the glass. He thumbed through the recent calls on his cell phone and found the number for The Voice. Vic hit *call* and listened to it ring once, twice, and then three more times before the ringing stopped. There was no voice mail. He poured himself a double whiskey and drank it down in one shot. Then he grabbed the towel from over his belt and frantically rubbed the top of his bar.

CHAPTER TWENTY-TWO

Patty and Rick headed south to Brookings. "Let's use Highway 5," she said. "I want to drop into the Medford Barnes & Noble. It's too early to visit the one here in Eugene."

"You realize Medford is out of our way, right?"

"Yeah, but it's only an extra thirty miles."

"Are you looking for a particular book?" asked Rick.

"I am. I'm reading a great murder mystery series and need the most recent one. I also need a gift for Mom. Her birthday's coming up."

"Is this another one of those gift stores you stick in that imaginary tool belt you've mentioned?"

"It is. You should come in with me."

Rick looked at Patty who was staring at him. She had a big smile on her face.

"I will. I'll browse the store while you search for your murder mystery and a gift for your mom."

Patty's cell phone interrupted the conversation, and she glanced at the caller ID. "Speaking of my mom."

"Detective O'Toole," she answered.

"Hello, Detective O'Toole. This is your mother. Have I told you lately how proud I am to have a daughter who is a detective? A true heroine of the northwest?"

Patty smiled. "You have, Mom, and I greatly appreciate your support."

"Well, I just don't want you to forget it. I also called to remind you that Bill and I leave tomorrow for our vacation."

"I remember, Mom. I planned to give you a call this evening. Rick and I are on our way back from Eugene."

"Eugene?" Maggie said. "This must have something to do with that big case. You figure out yet who did it?"

"Not yet. We're still in the investigative stage."

"Got any suspects? Is the killer from Eugene? Have you arrested anyone?"

"We're working on it, Mom. I can't give you any more information at this time. How about your vacation? Are you and Bill all packed? It must be exciting to know that in a couple of days you'll be riding on a train."

"We're packed and ready to go. It's very exciting. I hope we see lots of bison, bears, and big cats."

Patty laughed. "Big cats? I'm sure you'll see bison and elk. Possibly even a bear or two. But I doubt you'll find many big cats."

"Not a problem. We'll enjoy watching whatever we see."

"I read your itinerary and it looks wonderful. I'll enjoy hearing all about your trip when you get back. Is Bill as excited as you are?"

"I think so. He's feeling so much better that he's not worrying about the fatigue. His last PSA test showed his numbers low enough that they're not detectable on the testing equipment. He'll need to rest more frequently than before his surgery, but frankly, so do I. On another subject, Patty, I read in this morning's paper about the incident at McDonald's with the old man and some punks. Were you and Rick there?"

"We were not, Mom. Brad and Pete answered the call. I did hear the call come in from dispatch. An older guy was holding three young men at gunpoint. Brad said that when he and Pete got there, the old man had the three younger guys on the floor with their hands over their heads. There was coffee and breakfast spilled all over the table where the old man had been sitting. Brad noticed what appeared to be pancakes and syrup smeared on the guy's shirt too. Brad asked the old guy to lay his gun down on the table, which he did. As soon as the old man put his gun down, one of the young guys started to get up. Pete stopped that and ordered them all to remain. The old man explained that he'd just sat down to eat his breakfast when the three punks started harassing him. They asked for his wallet, and when he wouldn't give it to them, one of the punks picked up the old guy's coffee cup and poured it over his breakfast and onto the table. They then picked up the old guy's plate and smeared pancakes and syrup across his chest. Brad asked if any of the other patrons has seen what had happened, and several corroborated the old man's story. Pete cuffed the three guys on the floor, and he and Brad took them in."

"What about the old guy?" asked Maggie.

"Let me finish, Mom. Before Brad and Pete left, Brad shook the old man's hand and handed his .45 back to him. Brad said everyone in the McDonald's then broke out in applause."

"I'm so proud of our local law enforcement," said Maggie. "Tell Brad and Pete for me."

"I'll do that. You know, incidents like that take place around the country every day. We just don't hear about the times when firearms are used for personal protection."

"It would be good for more people to hear these stories. Bill and I can't physically defend ourselves anymore. Owning a 1911 and learning how to shoot has certainly increased my self-confidence. The world would be a safer place if more law-abiding citizens carried firearms."

"I'm glad that your training has helped you to be more comfortable in your home, Mom. You should target-shoot at least four or five times a year to remain confident in your ability to use your 1911. How about I take you and Bill out to shoot when you return from your trip?"

"We'd like that. Just let us know when you have time. Well, I'd better get back to preparing for tomorrow. Tell Rick I said hello."

"Will do, Mom. I'll call you when I get home. Love you."

"Love you too, dear."

Patty ended the call and Rick looked over at her. "How are your mom and Bill?"

"They're both well and looking forward to their trip. You should read the itinerary. They'll see several national parks and monuments in a relatively short period of time."

"Sounds like your mom wants to shoot too."

"Yeah. I want her to maintain her confidence in handling a firearm. She can do that best by practicing several times a year. Bill will shoot too. Want to join us?"

"I do," said Rick. "I was just talking to Barbara about her getting a pistol."

"Oh," said Patty. "You've seen Barbara again?"

Rick kept his eyes on the road. "Not seen her. But we spoke on the phone last night. We're going out to dinner again this weekend."

"Well, that's nice. I guess her work has slowed down."

"I don't know if it's slowed down or she just figured out how to better manage her time."

"Well, I hope it works out for both of you."

"We'll see."

* * *

The detectives returned to their office and each prepared to leave for home. Patty's cell phone rang, and she glanced at caller ID. "It's the lab," she said.

Rick sat down and waited to hear the news.

"Thanks," Patty said after jotting down a few notes. She looked up at Rick. "Vic's prints on the photo match those on the beer equipment in the storage unit."

Rick nodded his head. "He lied to us when he said that he hadn't stored the equipment there. He also lied about his relationship with David Dorisko."

Patty picked up a pencil and pulled a lined yellow pad in front of her. "So, let's look at Vic Thompson in relation to the others. Could he have killed Heising?"

"He knew Suzie Mantis," Rick said, "and he knows David Dorisko. My guess is he also knew Heising. What would be his motive for murdering Heising?"

"Drugs?" asked Patty. "He said he hadn't used for three years, but he could have been lying about that too!"

"And even if he isn't using, he could be dealing," Rick said. "He was uncomfortable when we spoke with him about Suzie's accident. Said he didn't like her, but what reason would he have for wanting her dead?"

"Let's give that some thought," said Patty. "He's got an alibi for the accident, but he may know who did it. Seems we've still got a lot more questions than answers. Let's talk with David Dorisko again. He may be concerned about the likelihood of his spending the next few years in a cell."

Rick stood up and put his jacket on. "It's been a long day and it's late. Okay with you if we continue this tomorrow morning?"

Patty nodded. "I'm beat too. See you in the morning. I'll be dropping Mom and Bill off at the airport in Crescent City before coming in."

"Tell them I'm looking forward to hearing about the trip," said Rick.

Rick left and Patty picked up her coffee cup. The cup had been a gift from her daughter eight years prior. Black lettering on the cup read *World's Greatest Mom*. Patty thought of the Deboes, picked up her cell phone and called Becky.

"Hi, Mom," Becky greeted her.

"Hi, Bec. How's your day been?"

"Same as always, Mom. Yours?"

"Rick and I are slowly making progress on our case."

A few moments passed in silence. "So, Mom, was there anything you wanted to talk about?"

"I just wanted to thank you again for the *World's Greatest Mom* coffee cup you gave me, and to tell you that I'm very proud to be your mother."

"Thanks, Mom. That works both ways you know. It's been awhile since I gave that cup to you. Did something happen today that made you think about it?"

"I don't know. Well, maybe. Your grandmother called me today. I was thinking about how much I appreciated my mom, and I was touched all over again when I remembered how meaningful it was when you gifted me with the cup. It's so special that I'm going to look for one on the internet to give to your grandmother for her birthday in a couple of weeks. I think she'll enjoy it as much as I've enjoyed this one from you."

"Grandma's birthday! Oh, my gosh! I forgot! I would have felt terrible if I'd let such a special day pass without wishing her a happy birthday."

"It's not a problem, Bec. You still have two weeks."

"Yeah, but I feel bad for almost forgetting. I've been preoccupied with school and Josh. I'm glad you reminded me. I'd better get back to my home-work. Are you still at work?"

"Yes. Rick's already gone home. I'll be leaving soon."

"You should put your work away and come home now, Mom. You sound tired."

"Thanks, Bec. I'll be there soon.

* * *

The next day, Patty saw Maggie and Bill off at the airport before arriving at the office.

"Good morning," she greeted Rick.

"Hey," he said. "I'm just finishing up a report. There's a doughnut in there if you want one." He pointed to the familiar-looking bag.

"Thanks. I'll get coffee first. Need a refill?"

Rick picked up his cup and stretched out his arm without looking up from his desk. "Thanks."

Thirty minutes later Rick finished his report. "So, are we going to inter-view Dorisko tomorrow?"

"I just called PO Lincoln, and she'll let the jail deputies know we'll be there. I told her I'd text our estimated time of arrival to her tomorrow morn-ing when we leave. I've been thinking more about Dorisko and his relation-ship with the others. What if Dorisko is blackmailing Vic? Vic claims to want nothing to do with Dorisko, but we know that he made bail for Dorisko the first time he was brought in."

"So you're suggesting that Vic's done something Dorisko's holding over him?"

"Yeah," said Patty. "It's a possibility."

"Now that you mention it, what if Dorisko has something on Suzie too? They all seem to be hiding secrets."

Patty's cell phone rang, and Rick listened as she responded to the caller with some excitement. "That's great. Our plan is to be there about noon tomorrow and interview her at one." She ended the call and saw Rick eagerly waiting to hear the good news.

"It's Suzie. She's awake and talking!"

CHAPTER TWENTY-THREE

"I'll let the LT know that our suspect is awake," said Patty. "He may suggest we leave now so that we can interview her as soon as possible."

"Come in, O'Toole," the lieutenant welcomed Patty when she walked up to his door. "What's the latest on your case?"

"We just got a call from the hospital in Eugene. Our suspect, Suzie Mantis, involved with dealing to June Deboe, has come out of her coma. Rick and I need to interview her, and we're thinking that we should complete our questioning as soon as possible, given her fragile condition. We could get to Eugene by four if we leave now. We also have an appointment set up early afternoon tomorrow to talk with Dorisko."

The lieutenant sat quietly for a minute. "What do you expect to get from Mantis?"

"We want to confront her about drug dealing to June Deboe, and ask about her relationship with Dorisko, Heising, and Thompson. One or more of them knows who killed Heising and why June was killed."

"Have you considered," the lieutenant asked, "that if someone intentionally tried to kill Mantis, that person is still at large and there may be others? Have you spoken with Eugene PD about her safety?"

"We have. She's had twenty-four-hour security at her hospital room since admittance. I haven't spoken with Strand about need for a safe house. Frankly, no one expected her to survive. She's beaten the odds on that count."

"I agree that you and Rick should leave now. I also think you should talk with Strand about Mantis' safety when she leaves the hospital. It may not be an issue if she admits to selling drugs to college students. If that's the case, she'll soon become a guest of the state in a very secure facility."

"We'll do that," Patty said. She walked back to her office and filled Rick in on the lieutenant's response.

"The LT agrees we should leave today. I need to run home and grab a few things. How about we meet back here in forty-five minutes?"

"I'll be here," said Rick.

Patty and Rick met up as planned, and Rick drove north on Highway 101. A little more than an hour later, he slowed down as they entered the town of Langlois. He read the sign on the side of the road. "Welcome to World Famous Langlois."

Patty laughed. "For a town of less than two hundred residents, that's a pretty bold sign."

Rick glanced over at Patty. "Well, you're the one who seems to know everything about Oregon. Why is Langlois world-famous?"

"I do know something about Langlois. And, since you asked, the name is pronounced phonetically, like 'Langless,' according to the town's written history. They pride themselves on several tourist attractions here in town including the Langlois Market, where you can find their world-famous hot dogs. Also of interest is that two electric companies serve residents of Langlois, depending upon where you live. The residents are served by both Coos-Curry Electric Cooperative and Bandon Electric."

"I wonder how many cities or towns can claim to have two different electric companies?" Rick asked.

"Probably not many. The city of Bandon first used steam-generated electricity for lights in 1907. About fifteen years later, the city began using hydropower. A hydroelectric plant was built on Willow Creek, south of Langlois, and a dam was constructed."

"Why did they change to purchasing power from Bonneville Power Administration?"

"Good question," said Patty. "Their hydroelectric plant didn't generate enough to meet the growing demand."

Rick's cell phone interrupted the conversation, and he checked caller ID. "It's Barbara," he said and answered the call. Patty couldn't help but overhear.

"Hi, Barbara. Tomorrow night? No, no. I didn't forget. It's just that I'm working on the case I told you about. Patty and I are on our way to Eugene now to question a suspect. We'll have to stay over tonight and continue working through some time tomorrow. I don't know if I'll be back in time to go to dinner. Can we make it Sunday instead? Oh, well, I understand. I'll call you when I get back and we'll pick another evening to go out. What? This is my job. Okay, we'll talk when I get back."

* * *

The hospital was quiet when Rick and Patty arrived. Suzie Browne Mantis was on the third floor. They exited the elevator and knew immediately which room was hers by the uniformed officer sitting outside her door.

The detectives introduced themselves and showed their credentials before going in. The woman they'd spent so much time trying to locate lay on her back in a sterile hospital room. She had two IVs in her arm, bandages around her head, and both an arm and a leg in casts. Her eyes were closed as Patty walked up next to the bed.

"Suzie Mantis?" Patty asked.

Suzie's eyes remained closed.

"Suzie Mantis?" Patty said a little louder.

Patty saw Suzie's eyelashes flutter, and she slowly opened her eyes. "Suzie, my name is Detective O'Toole. I need to ask you some questions."

Suzie gave no indication that she was comprehending Patty's words.

"Do you know who did this to you?"

When Suzie didn't respond, Patty continued. "Do you know that June Deboe was murdered?"

Suzie's eyes now darted around the room. She fought the restraints around her arms that had kept her from getting out of bed. A nurse opened the door and stepped in.

"Who are you?"

Patty and Rick introduced themselves, showed their credentials, and explained why they were there.

The nurse did not reciprocate by introducing herself. Instead, she pointed toward the door. "I can't have you upsetting my patient. She just woke up from a coma and needs to remain calm. I'm sorry, but you'll both have to leave."

"We need answers," said Patty. "And we have a few more questions."

"Alright," said the nurse, "but if your questions result in further upsetting my patient, I'll have to demand that you leave the room."

Patty looked back at the patient. "Suzie, we know that you were selling drugs to June Deboe. We also know that you had a relationship with David Dorisko, Howard Heising, and Vic Thompson. We think that someone hired by Dorisko or Thompson tried to kill you. We can't keep you safe unless you tell us why they'd want to kill you. What is the link between the four of you?"

Suzie looked at Rick and then back to Patty. She began to tremble. "Dorisko," she said. "He wants to kill me."

Before Patty could continue, the patient began having difficulty breathing, and the nurse asked the detectives to leave.

They left and started back toward the elevator.

"She knows the answers to my questions," said Patty, "but she may be too scared to talk."

"And rightfully so," said Rick. "When word gets out that she's awake, somebody may attempt to finish the job. There seems to be a lot of animosity among this group of individuals. There's more going on here than just the drug dealing, and I'm guessing that Dorisko and/or Thompson are worried about what she'll say."

"Let's try again tomorrow," said Patty. "We'll keep it quiet as long as we can. Let's go talk with Dorisko."

* * *

David Dorisko's hands were secured to the table, and he seemed calm when Patty and Rick walked into the drab interview room at the county jail. The walls were gray and, other than the table and three chairs, the room was empty. A one-way window let the suspect know that he was being watched.

"Do you remember the rights we explained to you?" asked Rick.

"Yeah. I remember them."

"You look tired," said Rick. "Not sleeping well?"

Rick continued, hearing no response from Dorisko, "Suzie Mantis is in a coma after someone tried to remove her by plowing into her car. We believe you know who it was."

Still no response.

"You'd better start talking to us," Patty said, "if you ever want to sleep through the night again."

Dorisko lifted his head. "I heard about Suzie, but I didn't have anything to do with that."

Patty and Rick glanced at each other. "So you do know Suzie," said Patty.

"For too long," replied Dorisko.

"Let me guess," Patty said. "You two met in college. Laney College."

It appeared that Patty's comment hit a nerve in Dorisko. He paled and lost the sneer that had been on his face. "I'm not answering any more of your questions."

"You don't have to talk to us," said Patty, "but we're getting close, and you know it.

You, Heising, Thompson, and Mantis all went to Laney College together. Heising is dead, and there's been an attempt on Mantis' life. We think you're behind both events, and it's only a matter of time before we have the evidence that proves it."

Dorisko sat up straight, the fear evident in his eyes. "I'm telling you it wasn't me. I might have known those people, but I didn't kill Howard or try to kill Suzie."

The detectives stood up to leave.

"Sweet dreams, Dorisko," said Rick.

CHAPTER TWENTY-FOUR

Patty and Rick walked out of the county building and back to their car.

"I think we need to look at Vic Thompson's phone," said Patty. "He's involved with either the death of Heising or the accident or both. We need to know who he's been talking with. I'll ask Strand if he can write up a search-warrant affidavit for us."

Patty called Strand and went over the reasons for the warrant that he could provide to the judge. "Thompson's prints were on equipment in the storage unit where a double homicide took place and a kilo of coke was found. The coke was found in equipment belonging to Thompson. He knew Heising, and he knows Mantis well enough to exchange text messages. We need to confirm the reason for his relationship with Dorisko and find out whether there are text messages on his phone that will reveal information about either the murders or the accident."

"That should be enough," said Strand. "I'll write it up now and get it over to the judge."

"Great," said Patty. "In addition to the cell phone, include his house, car, all electronics, and the Bayou Lounge in its entirety."

Forty-five minutes later, the detectives met up with Strand at the Eugene PD.

"The judge was in his chambers," said Strand. "He agreed to all that we asked for. I've got a couple of officers at Thompson's house. They'll make sure no one goes in or out until we can search it."

"Thanks," said Patty. "Rick and I will go to the lounge. We'll seize the cell phone, search Thompson's car, and take his house keys. We'll meet your officers at the house."

Vic was sharing stories at the bar when Patty and Rick walked in. He looked up and panned the room, concerned that one or more of his customers might discern that, even in plain clothes, two cops had just entered the bar. One couple at a corner table stood up and left. Vic folded his arms across his chest as the detectives walked up to the bar. "I told you that unless you had a warrant, I didn't want you in here."

Rick handed the warrant to Vic while Patty reached over the bar and picked up Vic's phone.

"You can't take that. That's my business phone."

"Read the warrant," said Patty. "We also need the keys to your house and car."

"My house and car? Why?"

"Read the warrant," Patty repeated. "Now give us the keys or we'll get them ourselves."

Vic handed Patty his house key and car fob. Rick took the car fob. "Where's it parked?" he asked.

"On the street."

Rick wrote out a receipt and handed it to him before the detectives walked out with the key fob and Vic's cell phone.

The barmaid hurried across the room to the bar. "What's going on, Vic? First Lorin left you and now the cops are taking your keys. Do I need to be worried about my job?"

Vic stared at the woman. "Just serve the customers," he said.

Vic's car was parked in front of the lounge. It was a newer Ford 150 and was clean except for an empty McDonald's soft drink container in the cup holder. Patty opened the center console, where she found a flashlight, container of hand sanitizer, pen, and small notepad. A phone number on the notepad caught her eye so she tore off the top sheet. When they finished searching the truck, she and Rick drove to Thompson's house.

A squad car was parked at the curb as Rick pulled into the driveway. Thompson's was one of four addresses associated with an older house. "I'll bet these houses were pretty nice when built as single-family homes," he said. "It looks like they've all been converted into separate apartment units."

"It is beautiful architecture," said Patty, "but this one must have cost a small fortune to maintain as a single-family home. It's probably a cash cow, broken up into several units. Looks like Vic lives on the upper floor."

The detectives and two Eugene PD officers walked through the unlocked common front door and climbed the two flights of stairs to Vic's apartment door. Patty stepped out of the way and Rick knocked.

"Police," he said loudly. "We have a search warrant. Open the door." Hearing no response, he knocked and called out again before they entered the apartment and split up.

"I'll take the kitchen," said Patty. "Rick can take the living room, and you guys can each search a bedroom."

After opening several cupboards and the refrigerator, Patty noticed a small calendar attached by a magnet to the side of the refrigerator.

"Hey, Rick," she said. "Look at this."

Rick walked in and Patty showed him the calendar that had circles around three dates.

"Look at the dates he's circled."

Rick took a minute to look at the calendar. "The date Mantis was hit and the day after. He's also written 1K on each of those dates."

Patty pointed at the notes on the bottom of the calendar.

"It looks," said Rick, "like he wrote down 2K and then crossed it out."

"Because she didn't die?" asked Patty.

"That could be one interpretation."

The detectives looked at each other. "He hired someone to kill her," said Patty. "Let's go back to the PD and go through his phone."

Before leaving, Patty spoke to the Eugene officers. "You guys can finish the search and leave a copy of the warrant."

At the PD Patty began thumbing through Vic's text messages. "I'll give you numbers," she said to Rick, "and you can begin making a list of each with the associated dates." Forty minutes later, she'd called out numbers, times and dates for a couple dozen calls. "There's one number here that matches the one on the piece of paper I took out of Vic's truck. Why don't we start with it? You make the call. Maybe whoever it is will think you're Vic and provide some information."

Rick tapped the number into Vic's cell phone. It rang once before the call was picked up.

"Yeah?"

"What happened?" Rick asked.

"I don't know."

"I paid you," Rick said

"And you still owe the rest. She's in a coma and close to dead now. Wait a few more days."

"I will. I lost your address. I need it again in order to send the money."

Rick heard nothing but breathing for the next five seconds. He looked at Patty and shook his head. They both knew what was coming.

The sound of the voice was angry. "Who is this?"

"It's Detective Starker. We've got you."

Rick heard a click as the call ended.

"I'll call Strand," said Patty. "Thompson will have no choice but to run."

Patty's phone illuminated with a call. It was one of the two officers who remained at Thompson's house. "We found something in the bedroom trash that might be helpful. A PO box number written on a piece of paper."

"That's good work," Patty said. "Give me the number, and Rick and I will go to the post office. If it's a local box, we should get a name and street address to go with it."

There was a small crowd waiting in line to pick up or drop off packages when the detectives walked up to the counter. They waited for the customer being helped to complete her transaction and then asked to talk with the manager. The customers standing in line were talking among themselves, wondering what was going on.

The manager quickly walked out from the back room and up to the counter, where Patty briefly explained what they needed and why. The manager took the PO box number and left the counter. Within minutes he returned with a name and street address.

Patty called the information in to Strand. "The guy Thompson hired is Lyle Cooper. We're heading to his place now. Can you provide us with backup?"

"I'll send a couple of officers. We've picked up Thompson and will hold him here for a few hours."

"Good," said Patty. "We'll talk to him after we pick up Cooper if he hasn't already run."

Rick pulled into an old trailer park off the main highway. "I don't see addresses on every trailer," Patty said. "Several look vacant. According to the PO box, his trailer number is five. Let's drive to the end and park."

The area around the trailers was unkempt. Several overflowing garbage cans, a few cars missing tires, and a number of other objects no longer cared for were strewn across several yards. A couple of mangy-looking dogs wandered around off leash.

Two marked Eugene PD cars pulled off the highway and into the park. Rick rolled down his window and spoke to the officers. "It's the trailer at the end. You guys cover the back in case he tries to flee out a window. We'll go in through the front."

Rick stepped ahead of Patty and knocked on the trailer door. "Police," he hollered. "Open the door." The detectives drew their guns.

Rick turned the doorknob and found it unlocked. He looked at Patty. "Anything we find will be inadmissible, but we can always freeze the scene if we come across something, and then apply for the warrant."

The smell of pot was overwhelming as they walked in and slowly made their way through the trailer.

"He must have left right after you spoke with him," Patty said. "He ate only half his sandwich and his coffee cup is still a little warm. Let's find out who he pays space rent to. They may have a car license number to give us. Strand can put out a BOLO and write up a warrant to search this place."

The detectives thanked the officers, and Patty let them know about the intended BOLO.

"We'll knock on a few doors. See if anyone knows the make and color of his car."

Patty and Rick split up. Rick got lucky with the first trailer when a sixty-something middle-aged woman opened the door.

"You must be a cop," she said.

"You're right," said Rick. "I'm Detective Starker."

The woman leaned against the door frame with her arms crossed across her chest. "I watched you and that female cop go next door." She pointed to Cooper's trailer. "He left in a hurry a while ago."

"Any idea where he went?" asked Rick.

"Me? Not a chance. He looks and acts mean. Even kicked one of the dogs once for no reason at all. Made the dog yelp. No, I don't talk to him."

"What about his car? Can you describe it?"

The woman smiled. "You gonna put out one of those be-on-the-lookout bulletins for the car?"

Rick smiled back at her. "We are. How'd you know about a BOLO?"

She laughed. "I watch TV crime shows," she said. "You want to come in?"

"No, but thank you," said Rick. "So, about your neighbor's car."

"It's a Ford F-150 pickup. A dark blue one. Much nicer than the van he just sold."

"Sold?" asked Rick. "How long ago did he show up with the new car?"

"Couple days. And before you ask me, I don't know what he did with the van. One day it was here and the next day it was gone."

"Can you describe the van?"

"Not much to say. It was white and had a window in the back."

Rick handed his card to the woman. "Thank you for your time. I'd appreciate your giving me a call if your neighbor comes home."

"I'll do that. I might even give you a call if he doesn't come home."

Rick smiled. "Have a good day."

"Mm-hmm. You too, Detective."

Rick caught up with Patty, who had knocked on the doors of several trailers and was making notes in her tablet. She looked up to see Rick with a big smile on his face. "You were certainly there for a while," she said. "I figured you'd found religion or something. She have any useful information?"

Rick laughed. "She did. Our suspect just got rid of a white van and purchased a new dark blue F-150. I'll let Strand know and ask if one of his officers could check with the local salvage yard to see if he dropped the van off. You get anything?"

Patty pointed to one of the trailers. "The guy living there told me about the white van. He looks to be about eighty. He said that he's afraid of our suspect. Cooper once threatened to push the old guy over while in his wheelchair if he didn't keep his dog tied up. I'll call in the BOLO on our way back to the PD."

Patty and Rick arrived at the Eugene PD and were met by Strand. "Thompson was in the back room of his bar getting ready to run. You want to take the lead on his interview?"

"Thanks," said Patty. "You going to join us?"

"No. I'll watch and step in if I have a question you've not asked."

Patty nodded, and she and Rick walked down the hall. "I'll be good cop," she said.

Rick nodded. "That has a familiar ring to it."

Vic Thompson was slumped in the chair when the detectives walked in. His hands were cuffed to the table ring and folded as if in prayer. He had the look of a defeated man, never raising his eyes from the table when the detectives walked in and sat down.

"So," Patty said, "I'll bet you were more than just a little surprised to learn that Suzie Mantis is still alive."

"I don't know what you mean," said Thompson.

"I think you do. But before I go on, Rick is going to admonish you."

Rick pulled the small card from his pocket and read Thompson his Miranda rights. He agreed to talk.

"As I was saying," said Patty, "we know you're responsible for Suzie's accident because earlier today we spoke with the guy you hired to kill her."

Thompson looked up at Patty and all color drained from his face. After a pause, long enough to be suspicious, he shook his head. "Not me. That guy knows Dorisko. They planned it."

Patty glanced at Rick, letting him know to take over.

"You've got a calendar hanging on your wall. I'll bet if you try real hard, you can see it in your mind's eye. Do you see the circled dates?"

Thompson clamped his teeth but kept quiet.

"You made it easy for us, Thompson. You not only circled the dates but wrote in the dollar amount of the payments you made to have Mantis killed. Are you remembering? One thousand on the day she was supposed to die, another thousand the day after, and a couple more grand after that."

Vic looked up from the table. "That money had nothing to do with Suzie," he said. "I place bets on the horses and keep track of them on my calendar."

Patty sat forward and spoke softly. "We know who you hired, Vic. Detective Strand has officers bringing him in now. You might as well tell us you hired the guy. Try and save yourself or you're going to lose everything."

Thompson remained silent.

Patty and Rick folded their files. "Okay, Vic," Patty said, "we're done here. But be assured we've got enough evidence to put you behind bars for life. And it will be nothing like you enjoy behind your Bayou Lounge bar."

The detectives left the room and met up with Strand in his office.

"We need Cooper to talk," Patty said. "He'll give up Thompson, and we can play them against each other. Maybe then Thompson will give us names for those responsible for Heising's murder."

"We also need the van," said Strand. "It's critical to our case if it was used in the attempted murder of Mantis. I've got my officers checking salvage yards."

Patty looked at Rick and saw that he was beat. She then turned to Strand. "We've done all we can until you bring Cooper in. We'll get some sleep. Call us if you get him."

"I'll do that," said Strand.

CHAPTER TWENTY-FIVE

Patty looked at the clock. Two a.m. She leaned over and picked up her cell phone from where it vibrated on the bedside table. "O'Toole."

"O'Toole, this is Strand. We've got Cooper."

"Have you called Starker yet?"

"No."

"I'll call him," Patty said. "We'll be there in thirty minutes."

On the drive to the PD, Patty and Rick discussed the questions they would ask.

"We know from Thompson's cell phone," said Patty, "that he and Cooper communicated on several occasions, including both the day of and the day following the attempt to kill Mantis. We know from your conversation with Cooper on the phone that he was paid by Vic for something."

"And," said Rick, "we need to know what his ties are with David Dorisko, and whether Dorisko controls Thompson. If Thompson hired Cooper to kill Suzie, was Cooper also hired to kill Heising?"

They arrived at the PD and found Strand in the conference room with his lieutenant and two sergeants.

"Where'd you find him?" Patty asked.

"He'd driven as far as Grants Pass," said Strand, "and checked into a Best Western. Grants Pass PD spotted the car."

One of the sergeants called out to Rick and Patty, "There's doughnuts and coffee in the break room."

Rick glanced at Patty. "Coffee would be great," she said.

Rick returned with a coffee mug in each hand. He'd wrapped a couple of doughnuts into napkins and put them in his jacket pockets. He pulled out a chocolate-covered one and offered it to Patty.

"Thanks," she said before taking a bite. She enjoyed the moment, swallowed, wiped her mouth with a napkin, and turned her attention to Strand. "Cooper is your arrest for the hit-and-run that happened on your turf. How do you want to do this?"

"We were discussing that," said Strand. "We haven't found his van yet, so we have no weapon. We do believe he intentionally hit Mantis, but we have no proof that he intended to kill her. We've got the cell phone communications between Cooper and Thompson, but only evidence of phone calls. No texts. And then we have his brief conversation with Rick. We know that Thompson circled key dates on his calendar and wrote down dollar amounts, but without having something that connects that directly to Cooper and the accident, it won't hold up. I'm thinking we need more evidence. Something that can't be refuted."

"Do you think we have enough for a search warrant?" Patty asked.

"I do," said Strand. "But I think it best to wait a few hours so that we don't have to wake up the judge to get it."

"Then let's hold off questioning Cooper until we have the warrant and can search his trailer. We might find evidence that tells us where he hid his van."

"That makes sense to me," said Strand.

Patty nodded. "Rick and I will try talking with Mantis again while we wait for the warrant. Give me a call when you have it and we can meet you at Cooper's trailer."

* * *

Suzie Mantis was awake when the detectives walked in.

"Hello, Suzie," said Patty. "I'm Detective O'Toole and this is Detective Starker. We spoke with you yesterday. Do you remember?"

"No," she quietly replied.

"We want to talk with you about the cause of your accident. Is that okay?"

"Yes."

"Did you see the car that hit you?"

"No. I can't remember anything about the accident. Do you know who hit me?"

"We're working on that," said Patty. "We believe someone intentionally rammed your car with the intent to kill you."

Suzie closed her eyes for a few seconds.

"Suzie," Patty said, "when we spoke with you yesterday, you said that David Dorisko was trying to kill you. Do you still believe that?"

Suzie quietly stared at Patty before speaking. "I don't know why I said that."

Rick stepped up next to Suzie's bed. "We believe," he said, "that whoever tried to kill you is going to try again. You've had a police officer guarding the door to your room since the accident. But you'll soon go home, and we can't protect you if you won't cooperate with us."

Tears filled Suzie's eyes. "I don't know for sure that it was David."

"What about Vic Thompson?" asked Patty.

Suzie scrunched her eyebrows. "Vic? Vic wouldn't hurt me. He's just a friend."

"We have evidence, Suzie, that Vic hired the guy who crashed into you."

Suzie stared at Patty and then Rick. "Vic?" she asked again. "But why?"

"That's what we're hoping you can tell us," said Patty. "Do you know something about Vic that could get him into trouble with the law?"

Suzie slowly moved her head back and forth. "You're wrong about Vic. He wouldn't hurt me."

Patty glanced at Rick and then looked down at Suzie. "What do you know about Vic and David Dorisko that they don't want you talking about?"

Suzie said nothing.

"Suzie," said Rick, "we think that you, Vic, and David are involved in something more than drugs. They're not going to defend you if they can save themselves by giving you up. You need to start talking to us."

Patty's cell phone pinged with a call. "It's Strand," she said before answering and stepping out of the room.

Strand sounded excited. "We found the van."

"Where was it?"

"Not far from where he lives. About twenty feet off the main road and covered up with tree branches. It's clear that it's been in an accident. We have forensics working on it now. They've already found paint on the front bumper that matches the color of the Mantis car. I'll write up the warrant affidavit and ask if the judge will approve it over the phone."

"Make sure you include all electronics and indicia of occupancy," said Patty. "We want to look through everything. We now have the proof we need that it was Cooper's van that hit the Mantis car. We'll also prove that Cooper drove it if his are the only fingerprints on the steering wheel. We still need some solid evidence that it was Thompson who hired Cooper. That will give us leverage to get Thompson to talk about the Howard Heising murder. Rick and I will stay here at the hospital for a while. This new information should leave no question for Mantis that one or more people want her dead. And that should make her more fearful than the idea of going to prison for the drug dealing."

Patty entered Suzie's room again to find the patient much more nervous than she'd been when they left her. She was awake and had been crying from the look of her red, wet eyes.

Patty looked at Rick and then Suzie. "Eugene police have found the van that hit you. And we know that it was Thompson who hired the driver with the intent to have you killed."

Suzie's mouth fidgeted, and she bit her lower lip as she paused before speaking. She looked up at the detectives. "All right."

Patty and Rick glanced at each other, and Rick pulled out his pad and pen. They both quietly waited for Suzie to go on.

"I dealt drugs. I've been dealing for a long time. I sold drugs to college students and got a few of them to work for me on campus."

"We know about the drugs," said Patty. "We know that June Deboe was working for you."

"Not for very long," said Suzie. "She was just some dumb kid who thought she was smarter than all of the information she'd heard from others about the dangers of drugs. She kept telling me that she just wanted to pay off her student loans and then she was going to quit. They all say something like that."

"How does Vic Thompson fit into this?" asked Patty. "What is it he doesn't want you talking about?"

Suzie looked around the room and then back at Patty. "He was dealing with me when we were in college. We were together then. You know what I mean? Vic met June when she temporarily worked for him in the lounge during spring break. That's how I met and befriended her. She told me about attending College of the Redwoods and her school loans, and she was sure she'd never get them paid off. So I offered her a job selling for me on her campus. Vic became angry at me when he learned that I'd told June about the long-term drug business he and I had set up. He didn't want his girlfriend finding out that he was a drug dealer."

Patty looked at Rick, and he stepped forward. "So," he said, "Vic didn't want you talking about his past involvement with drugs. That's hardly a reason to try and kill you. I think there's more. What is it you're not telling us?"

"I wouldn't think that Vic would kill me over that either, but he really loves his girlfriend, and she has no idea about his past."

"Okay," said Patty. "What about Dorisko? Why would he want you permanently gone?"

"Pretty much the same reason," said Suzie. "Only he's still into drugs. He's been my supplier. Maybe he heard from Vic that I wanted to move and he's not going to let me out."

"You were going to move?" asked Patty. "Does your husband know this?"

"Tommy? No. And you can't tell him. He doesn't know about my dealing. Tommy's just a nice guy who works too hard. He's taken care of me and the kids because he wants to, but he doesn't really know me."

"If he didn't know," asked Patty, "why did he agree to move?"

"He didn't agree. We talked about it and I gave him a chance. But he's too tied to his job and doesn't want the kids to leave their friends. I figure that if he really loved me, he'd quit his job and sell the house so that we could all move away from here. I could have quit dealing."

Rick nodded. "So you were going to walk out on Tommy and your kids and take off on your own."

Patty glanced at Rick and then looked back at Suzie. "Who killed Howard Heising?"

"I don't know for sure. I wouldn't have thought that Vic had it in him to kill someone. But I guess maybe he did hire someone to try and kill me. So my money's on Vic for Howard's death. He either shot Howard or hired someone to kill him."

"Why would Vic want Howard dead?" asked Patty.

"I'm guessing," said Suzie, "that it was for the same reason he wanted to kill me. To shut Howard up. Oh, I guess I didn't mention it. Howard Heising was one of our college friends. He knew all about our drug lives."

"Did he use and sell too?" asked Patty.

Suzie moved her head back and forth. "Howard? No. He just hung out with us."

Patty's cell phone rang. It was Strand. "We've got the warrant."

"Great. We'll head over to his trailer now."

Patty ended the call and looked up at Suzie. "Are you sure that's all you want to tell us?"

"That's all I know," said Suzie.

During the drive to Cooper's trailer, Rick shook his head. "She's a piece of work."

"Yeah," said Patty, "and she's been living a double life."

The detectives opened every drawer and cupboard in Cooper's trailer, hoping to find something that linked Cooper to Thompson. Patty moved a few things on top of the kitchen counter. She heard a noise and took the lid off a coffee canister.

"In here, Rick," she called out.

Rick walked in and saw Patty holding a cell phone in one hand and a wad of papers in the other.

"A second phone," he said.

"And bank statements for the past couple of months," said Patty. "They show a thousand dollars was deposited into his account on each of the first two dates Vic circled on his calendar. Let's take this back to the PD and go through his phone."

Patty's cell phone rang, and she saw on caller ID that it was her mother. "It's Mom," she said to Rick.

Patty answered the phone. "Detective O'Toole."

"Hello, Detective O'Toole. This is your mother."

"Hi, Mom. Are you and Bill having a good time?"

"A marvelous time, dear. Today we saw the Yellowstone geysers."

"That's great, Mom. I want to hear more but I can't right now. Let me call you back, probably tomorrow."

"There must be something big going on with your case. Call me when you have time. You and Rick stay safe."

"Always, Mom." Patty ended the call.

Eugene PD provided the same room to the detectives that they'd worked in before. Rick looked through the cell phone messages between Cooper and Thompson while Patty called the lieutenant to give him an updated status on their case and actions. "I'll let him know we'll stay in Eugene tonight and leave in the morning for Brookings."

Rick continued flipping through messages on Cooper's phone. "Nothing so far but phone calls," said Rick. "I've gone back a couple of weeks. His phone calls to Vic coincide with the dates circled on Vic's calendar. No text messages."

Patty wrote down the phone numbers for Dorisko and Mantis and put them in front of Rick. "Put these numbers in his phone and see if there are communications with either of them."

Rick tapped in Dorisko's number. Patty watched him stop at one message.

"Listen to this," he said. "It's a text message from Cooper to Dorisko. *Thompson wants me to off the woman.* Then Dorisko tells Cooper, *Go ahead. She's no good to me anymore.* There's another here on the date Cooper attempts to kill Suzie. He texts Dorisko, *It's done.*"

"That, along with our other evidence," said Patty, "should be enough to get us a conviction. Let's talk with Strand."

They found Strand in his office. "This shouldn't be difficult," Strand said. "We've got enough to put Cooper away for attempted murder, and Thompson for ordering the hit. Do you still make Thompson for your homicide in the storage unit?"

"He's certainly a suspect," said Patty. "It could be that it was Cooper who did the job. Rick and I will talk about how we'll interview Thompson and let you know when we want to set it up. We need to head back to Brookings tomorrow."

"Thanks to both of you for your help," said Strand.

Patty's cell phone rang. She didn't recognize the number on caller ID and let it go to voice mail. "This has helped us too," she said to Strand. "It's interesting how it all came together. We may still have an interest in Cooper for the murder."

"Let me know if we can help."

Patty and Rick left the PD and drove back to their hotel. On the way, Patty checked the voice mail message that had been left. "Rick, this is a message from Laney College. It's the Admissions clerk I spoke with. I asked if there had been a memorable incident of any kind during the year Mantis, Dorisko, Thomas and Heising were there. She couldn't think of anything at the time of my call and said she'd talk with a few others who were working at the school during that year."

"Something happened?" asked Rick.

"That's what her message says. I'll try reaching her."

Patty's call went to voice mail. She left her name and number.

"They're closed today, so I'll try again tomorrow. What time do you want to leave tomorrow?"

"Let's make it early," said Rick. "About seven, if that works for you."

"Seven will work," said Patty.

CHAPTER TWENTY-SIX

The drive back to Brookings was easy with good weather and no roadwork delays.

"You spoke about electricity on the way up," said Rick. "What's your take on the rolling blackouts in California?"

"I think they're going to continue for years. I also think that those of us living in the Northwest may be introduced to the same thing."

"Us?" asked Rick. "Blackouts in Oregon? Why?"

"Because of the coal plants closing," said Patty. "Energy experts continue to study the possible effects of having a supply shortage for the increased demand when all twelve coal plants close within the next eight years. The combined energy of those coal plants electrifies close to four million homes."

"I had no idea there are that many homes in the Northwest that are energized by coal," said Rick. "How convinced are the experts that we'll experience blackouts?"

"According to some studies I've read, the probability exceeds 25% that by the year 2026 we may not have enough supply to meet the demand. Not having an adequate supply of energy could result in blackouts and/or a substantial increase in cost of electricity to the consumer."

"What about wind and solar?" asked Rick. "Shouldn't we be building more wind turbines and solar plants?"

"Wind and solar are great providers of electricity when they work, and Oregon has a lot of wind turbines along the Columbia Gorge east of Portland. They produce when the wind is blowing, but the wind doesn't always blow, and there's currently no way to capture that excess energy for use at some other time. As for solar, it too is unreliable, and we don't yet have the necessary battery storage."

"Why should we on the coast worry when we have hydro?"

"Hydro has its own problems with dependability. It's great as long as we don't experience a severe drought or remove essential dams."

"Is there any dependable source of electricity?"

"There's natural gas, but it has a carbon footprint about half that of coal. And there's nuclear."

"So," said Rick, "it seems we've got an impending problem."

"That's where we're at, according to what I've read. Renewables are great but unreliable. There are companies working hard on new technology to build batteries with a far greater storage ability than what we have today. The question is whether in six years, even with improved batteries, the supply will meet the demand."

"Possible electricity shortage in the Northwest. That's something I've never considered."

Nearing Brookings, Patty remarked, "Have I ever mentioned that I love our beautiful coastline?"

Rick smiled. "I'm in awe every time we take this drive. These magnificent sea stacks tell of such a unique geological history. Something you don't see along most of the US coastline, and one of the main reasons I decided to move here."

Ten minutes later, Rick pulled into the PD parking lot. Patty unbuckled her seatbelt. "You going to see Barbara tonight?"

Rick paused before answering. "No, she said she'd be busy writing up an offer."

"Oh," said Patty.

* * *

The following morning Patty called her mother. "Do you have time to talk?"

"I have a few minutes," said Maggie. "Bill and I are going to breakfast soon."

"What's on your trip agenda for today?"

"We're going to the Black Hills of South Dakota. We'll stop at Sturgis, where the annual motorcycle ride takes place. Lucky for us, the event will not be taking place while we're there."

"Have you learned yet," asked Patty, "why the hills are called the Black Hills?"

"I wondered too. I haven't heard yet on the tour, but I've read that it's the dark tree bark and Ponderosa pine needles that give the impression that the hills are black."

"Are you going to ask around while you're there? Find out if anyone knew my aunt or Cousin George?"

"I will," said Maggie. "Your aunt, your dad's sister, was a schoolteacher who taught both the whites and the Indians. She travelled back and forth to school on horseback. I remember hearing the story of her getting caught in a storm and suffering frostbite on both feet. Your cousin, George, left home as a young man. He briefly rode the rails and then joined the Navy. Last I heard, he had married a beautiful young woman and made the Navy a career."

"Seems we come from some pretty strong stock, Mom."

"We do," said Maggie. "Your relatives on both sides were hard-working people. They took care of their own with whatever they had. And I know, from stories handed down from one generation to the next, that most had very little."

"I'd like to meet some of them," said Patty. "Do you have any idea whether they stayed in South Dakota?"

"I'm sorry, dear, but I don't. Your dad's death was so sudden that it put me into a deep depression for a few years, and I lost touch with the few relatives I knew from his side of the family. I'll write down the relatives' names I remember and give them to you when we return."

"That would be great, Mom. Thanks."

"Bill is ready, so we're going to breakfast. I'll call in a couple of days."

"Okay. I hope the trip continues to be fun for you both."

"I'm sure it will. You and Rick stay safe. Love you."

"Love you too."

CHAPTER TWENTY-SEVEN

Patty was at her desk early, working on a report, when the Admissions clerk called.

"Detective O'Toole," she answered.

"Detective, this is Hazel in the Admissions Office at Laney College. You and I spoke about four students who were here fifteen years ago."

"Dorisko, Heising, Thompson, and Browne," said Patty.

"Well, you asked if I remembered any incident that may have occurred during the year those four were here."

"Have you thought of something?"

"I didn't, but I was asking my co-workers about it, and one of them remembered something that may be of interest to you."

"What's that?"

"A student went missing and has never been found."

"What would that have to do with the four people we discussed?" asked Patty.

"Well, two of them, Browne and Dorisko, were questioned more than once by the police. And the police asked us about them. Other students said that they thought Dorisko and Browne were suspects in the case. The student that went missing was using drugs, and more than one said they saw the missing student buying drugs from Suzie Browne."

"And," Patty said, "the missing student's never been found?"

"That's right, Detective. There was quite a flurry of action for the first few weeks and then nothing."

"Thank you, Hazel. This may turn out to be quite helpful."

Rick walked into the office yawning. "I'm getting too old for these six-day work weeks."

"Focus on the overtime," said Patty. "I need to tell you about the call I just had after you get your coffee."

Rick came back from the kitchen with coffee and a piece of cake. "Must be somebody's birthday. You'd better get yours now before it's gone."

"I already ate breakfast," said Patty.

Rick broke off a piece of cake with his fork and began bringing it up to his mouth. He stopped momentarily to respond to Patty. "What does that have to do with getting a piece of birthday cake before it's gone?"

Patty smiled. "I just got a call from Hazel, the Laney College Admissions clerk. Someone does remember an incident during the year our suspects attended. A student went missing. She was a drug user who bought from Suzie Browne, now Mantis. The same employee remembers that Browne and Dorisko were questioned. Other students mentioned they thought those two might be suspects."

Rick put his fork down. "That brings up a lot of possibilities. Could we be looking for a serial killer?"

"Could be, Rick. Let's call Oakland PD." Patty looked in the law enforcement directory for an Oakland detective, tapped the number into her cell phone, and put it on speaker. The call was picked up after two rings.

"Detective Thursday."

"Detective, this is Detective Patty O'Toole. I'm on the phone with Detective Rick Starker. We're with Brookings, Oregon PD."

"What can I do for you?" asked Thursday.

"We're investigating a double homicide," said Patty. "One of the victims and three of our suspects all attended Laney College in 2004. Three of these individuals are or have been involved with drug dealing. We've just learned that a Laney College student went missing in 2004, and that the missing student was involved with our suspects. We've also learned that two of our suspects were questioned by Oakland PD at the time the college student went missing."

"I was here in '04 and I remember the incident," said Thursday. "I'll need to pull the file if you want to ask questions."

"That would be appreciated," said Patty. "When do you think you'd have time to do that?"

"Give me a couple hours to finish the report I'm working on. I can tell you now that the body of the missing student has never been found."

"Two hours would be great. We'll wait for your call."

The call ended and Rick looked at Patty. "Is this what ties those four together? They were involved with the disappearance of another student?"

"It could be," said Patty. "We've been thinking that Heising's death had something to do with drugs. Maybe it had to do with the disappearance of the student. We've got a couple of hours. I'll let the LT know where we're at."

Patty walked down the hall to find the lieutenant at his desk.

"Come in, O'Toole," he said.

"We just learned," said Patty, "of a Laney College student's disappearance in 2004, the year our four suspects were also attending. Rick and I are now wondering if one or more of our suspects had something to do with the incident."

The lieutenant sat quietly considering the new information. Patty waited for his comments.

"That could be the reason for blackmail."

"Blackmail?" asked Patty.

"Yes," said the lieutenant. "You and Rick have wondered why Mantis hasn't given up Dorisko or Thompson. And why Dorisko won't give you anything on the others. If they're responsible for the missing student, they could all be bound to secrecy for fear of being discovered."

"The Heising death begins to make sense," said Patty. "He wasn't into the drug scene and may have unintentionally learned about the reason for the student missing. It's possible the others thought he was going to talk. But why would he kill June Deboe?"

"What did she know?" asked the lieutenant.

Patty's cell phone rang. "It's Detective Thursday," she said. "I'll need Rick to hear this and fill you in after the call."

The lieutenant nodded and Patty left his office.

She answered the call while walking back to her desk. "My partner's here. I'm going to put you on speaker. Can you tell us about the case?"

"It was your classic missing person's case at first," said Thursday. "The girl was eighteen and had been missing two days when her parents called. We took the usual precautions of assuming she ran away and put out a BOLO for her and her car. We found the car."

"Did you dust the inside of her car?" asked Patty.

"We did. Every inch of it. We found some prints for the girl, one of her friends, and a couple of other students attending Laney at the time."

"Do you have the names of those other students?"

"Yes. David Dorisko and Suzie Browne."

"Tell us about those two," said Patty.

"They both claimed to be fellow students of the girl. Said that she periodically gave each of them a lift to school. The thing is, my gut told me there was more."

"Why was that?" asked Patty.

"For one thing, they were both drug users and dealers known to several other students we spoke with. They had alibis for each other when asked about their whereabouts on the day the victim went missing, but neither had anyone to corroborate their stories."

"Anything else?" asked Patty.

"There was. Another student we questioned was extremely nervous when asked about Browne and Dorisko. He seemed to be afraid of them and refused to answer our questions about their contact with the missing girl. I remember thinking he was holding back."

"Do you remember that student's name?" asked Patty.

"I didn't until I reviewed the file. His name was Howard Heising."

Patty and Rick glanced at each other. "Heising is one of our double homicide victims," Patty said. "He was killed in a storage unit rented by David Dorisko's brother."

"You're thinking our cold case and your recent homicides could be related?" asked Thursday.

"After what you've just told us, we're sure they're related. Can you send us a copy of the file?"

"Sure. I'll have it scanned and sent right over. I'll also open the case again now that there's a chance you've found our responsible. I'd appreciate your keeping me abreast of your findings where they relate to our case."

"We'll do that," said Patty.

An hour later, Patty and Rick were reviewing the file at their desks.

"According to the girl's mother," said Patty, "the girl wore a birthstone necklace all the time. A ruby on a gold chain."

"A ruby?" asked Rick. "Why does that seem familiar?"

"You thinking of something in evidence?"

"No, but give me a minute."

Patty watched as Rick sat back in his chair and closed his eyes. A few minutes had passed when he opened his eyes and sat up. "I know where I saw a necklace like that. In the Bayou Lounge when we first spoke to Vic Thompson. There was a young woman sitting at the table to our left. She was talking with the barmaid at the time. I looked around the room and she was staring at us. She had a low neckline and wore a gold necklace with a stone on the end. The light was reflecting off it, and I'm sure the stone was a ruby. She was still sitting there by herself when we left. That made me think she was waiting for either Thompson or the barmaid."

"We need to talk with the barmaid," said Patty. "I'll let the LT know. We can go back to Eugene tomorrow." She left her desk and walked down the hall. When she returned, Rick was on the phone with Barbara.

"I know, Barbara, but this case has me tied up. I promise to make time for dinner as soon as I can."

Rick looked at Patty when he finished the call. Patty paused and then went back to the case. "The LT agrees that we need to get back to Eugene and talk with Thompson again. I'm going home now so that I can get some sleep before taking off again tomorrow. You might want to do the same."

"Works for me," said Rick.

CHAPTER TWENTY-EIGHT

The next morning Patty and Rick headed back up the coast.

"I heard that Hooskanaden is moving again," said Patty. "So you may want to slow down to about twenty-five when we get there."

Rick chuckled. "It's a pit into which the state continues to throw money. Like Devil's Slide used to be in California, before the state rerouted the highway. At some point, Oregon will have to do the same with the Hooskanaden stretch of 101. We don't want another slide like that in 2018 when the road dropped twelve feet in less than twenty-four hours."

"Don't hold your breath on it being rerouted," said Patty. "I think that option is cost-prohibitive."

The detectives arrived at Eugene's PD and briefed Strand on what had transpired.

"Before talking with Thompson, we want to meet with the girlfriend," said Patty. "The barmaid at Vic's lounge knows her. We'll start there."

When the detectives arrived at the Bayou Lounge, Rick recognized the barmaid he'd seen talking with the woman wearing a ruby necklace. They waited until she finished taking an order and then followed her to the bar.

Patty showed her identification. "We have a few questions for you. Is there a table we can sit at?"

"Yeah," she said, pointing to a corner table. "Over there. Let me take care of this order first."

The detectives walked to the table and sat down.

"What do you want?" the barmaid asked when she arrived.

"Do you recognize us?" asked Patty.

"Sure. You're the cops who came down on Vic. What's he done?"

Patty ignored the question and pointed across the room. "The first time we came in, you were talking to a young woman at the small table against that wall. Who was she?"

"Is she in trouble too?" asked the barmaid.

"We just want to know who she is."

"That was Lorin. Vic's girlfriend. Well, his former girlfriend. If she's in trouble, please don't tell her I gave you her name. I don't want any hassles. I just want to work and collect a paycheck."

"We understand," said Patty. "What's Lorin's last name?"

"Smith. Lorin Smith. I think she used to live with Vic, at least part of the time, but she's left him, and I don't know where she is."

"Okay," said Patty. "Thanks for your help."

Rick and Patty returned to the PD, where Patty used CJIS to obtain information on Lorin.

"This shouldn't take long," she said to Rick. "Was CJIS the acronym you used in Boston for your Criminal Justice Information Services?"

"It was. I think that the acronym stands for the same thing in most states. Did you know it's only been in place since 1992 and that it's now the largest division of the FBI?"

"I didn't. I've found it valuable, as I'm sure all agencies have. It's so easy to input a name and learn of criminal activities in local and international communities."

"It certainly has helped law enforcement," said Rick. "Before we had a centralized source of information there were situations where a criminal in one state moved to another and was able to start a whole new string of crimes because agencies in the newest state didn't know about the criminal's past behavior."

Patty glanced at her computer. "Here she is. Name, address, and phone number." Patty put her cell phone on speaker and tapped in Lorin's number.

"Hello?"

"Is this Lorin Smith?" asked Patty.

"It is. Who's calling?"

"Detectives O'Toole and Starker. We want to ask you a few questions about your relationship with Vic Thompson. Would you like to come down to the station or can we stop by your home?"

"You can come here," she said.

"Okay if we meet you in about fifteen minutes?"

"Sure."

The detectives arrived at Lorin's apartment, and she showed them into her living room, where they all took a seat.

"There isn't a relationship anymore," said Lorin. "He wasn't honest with me."

"How long have you known Vic?" asked Patty.

"About a year."

"Have you met his friends?"

"No. We never went out with anyone else. I just figured he was a hard worker because of all the hours he spent at the Bayou. He had no time for friendships."

"Lorin, do you have a necklace with a ruby on it?"

"I do. How did you know?"

"Where did you get it?" asked Patty.

"Vic gave it to me."

"We need to borrow it," said Patty. "We don't believe Vic purchased the necklace, and it may be part of a case we're working on."

"Oh, my God. First, he lies to me, and now you tell me that he didn't buy the necklace he gave me. Well, I don't want stolen jewelry. I'll get it from my jewelry box and give it to you."

"I'll go with you," said Patty. "If we find it wasn't stolen, we'll give it back to you."

Lorin gave the necklace to Patty, and the detectives drove back to the PD. Rick took photos of the necklace, then scanned and emailed them to Detective Thursday for confirmation. Ten minutes had passed when Rick's phone rang.

"This is it," said Thursday. "I emailed the photo to the girl's mother, and she confirmed that it's an exact match to her daughter's."

"That's great," said Patty. "This ties our current suspects to your missing person's case."

"I'd like to know if you get a confession at your end."

"We'll let you know," said Patty

After the call Patty picked up a pen and pulled a yellow tablet over in front of her. "So, we've got evidence that Thompson hired Cooper to kill Mantis. And that he stays in communication with Dorisko."

"And," said Rick, "we now have evidence that he was involved with the missing student cold case."

"His association with the cold case may be what brings him down," said Patty.

"It's interesting," said Rick, "that there's nothing in the file that suggests he was ever questioned. And no confirmation that his prints weren't in the car. So what did he have to do with the student's disappearance?"

The detectives were shown to an interview room where Vic Thompson was handcuffed and secured to the metal ring on the table.

"How you doing?" asked Rick.

Thompson stared at Rick and then slowly moved his eyes over to Patty. "I shouldn't be in here. Suzie knows I wouldn't hurt her. You've got the wrong guy."

"I don't think so," said Patty. "We've got a text message on Cooper's phone telling Dorisko that you wanted him to off Suzie Mantis. And we've got the dates and dollar amounts on your calendar matching deposits into Cooper's account. How long have you known Cooper?"

"I don't know anyone by the name of Cooper," said Vic.

"Well, he knows you. And he's ready to testify that you hired him to kill Suzie Mantis. He's ready to say whatever he needs to in order to get a reduced sentence. He has no problem selling you down the river."

Vic looked at the ceiling and then to the detectives. "She's not dead. So you can't hang a murder on me."

"Possibly not," said Patty. "Not Suzie's anyway."

"What do you mean?" asked Vic.

"We're talking about the college student who disappeared fifteen years ago when you, Mantis, Dorisko, and Heising attended Laney College together."

Vic furrowed his eyebrows. "What student? I don't know about any student who disappeared."

"You need to start being honest with us, Vic. You just keep digging the hole you're in deeper and deeper."

Patty took the photo out of her vest and laid it in front of Thompson. "Look familiar? How many gold-chain ruby necklaces have you seen, Vic? Your girlfriend gave us this one."

Vic began moving his head back and forth.

"The mother of that girl," said Patty, "the one who went missing, has confirmed that the necklace you gave to Lorin was her daughter's. So now we've got you on the attempted murder of Mantis and the murder of the student whose necklace you removed."

"I didn't kill her."

"Then you need to tell us what happened, because you're looking at twenty-to-life in a place I know you'd rather not be."

Vic laid his head down on his hands. "I didn't kill her."

Patty softened her voice. "Look, Vic. You've worked hard to get ahead after some bad years. You're a businessman, owning your own lounge. You're on a path to losing everything."

"I didn't kill her."

"You took her necklace," said Patty.

"Dorisko gave it to me. Told me it was valuable."

"Why'd Dorisko give it to you? Why not keep it for himself?"

"Because I helped bury her."

"The missing student?" asked Patty.

"Yes."

"Who killed her?" asked Patty.

"I don't know. Howard was crashing with me at the time, and Dorisko showed up one day saying he needed Howard and me to help him and Suzie with something. We went with him to an abandoned forest trail into the woods. We hiked for a while before Dorisko told us to stop. He stepped off the path and brushed some leaves from the girl's body. He told us to dig a hole and bury her."

"You didn't ask what happened?" asked Patty.

"No. I just helped. Dorisko gave me the necklace and I left."

There was a knock at the door and Thompson's attorney walked in. He looked at his client. "I told you not to talk to these guys without me."

"They're trying to pin a murder on me that I didn't commit. I want to know what I'd get in return for testifying against Dorisko."

The attorney looked at the detectives. "Can my client and I have a few minutes?"

"Sure," said Patty. She and Rick walked out and waited in the hallway.

Ten minutes later they were asked to return. The attorney spoke for Thompson. "All you have on my client is the attempted murder. He didn't drive the van that hit Mantis. He's told you he didn't kill the missing student, only that he helped to bury her."

"We're going to charge your client with attempted murder against Suzie Mantis and abuse of a corpse."

"My client hasn't killed anyone. But he believes Dorisko did. What if he agrees to testify against Dorisko? Will you drop the charges related to the fifteen-year-old case and give him leniency on paying to have Mantis killed?"

"Does your client have any proof it was Dorisko?" asked Patty.

The attorney looked at Thompson. "Tell them."

"Dorisko had blood on his clothes when he came over that day to get me and Heising. He said that he and Suzie had been hiking with the student. They all were high and pretty messed up. He said that the student started hallucinating and she ran. He said she fell and hit her head on a rock. He said it was an accident."

"Why do you think it wasn't an accident and that he killed her?" asked Patty.

"Because Suzie told me that the girl had been shot."

"You didn't come forward when the authorities were searching for her. Why?"

"Dorisko said he'd pin the murder on me if I ever said anything about it. I'd already had a brush with the cops and didn't want them looking at me for the murder. He convinced me to keep my mouth shut."

"Do you recall where the body is buried?" asked Patty. "Could you take us there from the college?"

"Yeah, I think I could."

Patty looked at Dorisko's attorney. "This is a multi-agency cooperation case. We'll talk with the Alameda County DA and get back with you."

The detectives left the room. "Let's talk with Dorisko," Patty said, "before I make my calls. We've got some leverage now."

Rick saw one of the officers come out of the kitchen with a doughnut. "While you arrange to have Dorisko brought over, I'll check out the doughnuts. Want one?"

"I could use the sugar and caffeine. I'll meet you in the kitchen in a few minutes."

Patty found Rick sitting at one of the tables opposite the coffee and pastries. He had a glazed doughnut in one hand and a mug in the other. She chose something that was chocolate-covered and poured black coffee into a Styrofoam cup. "We've got twenty minutes," she said. "We need to keep the momentum going."

"How do you want to do this?" Rick asked. "Good cop, bad cop?"

Patty nodded. "You start and I'll come in to let him know someone cares."

"Do you think Thompson was telling the truth?" asked Rick.

"Hard to tell," said Patty, "but I'm thinking he is. His fear of spending the rest of his life in prison is stronger than his fear of Dorisko."

"Dorisko's going to put the death back on Thompson."

"He is," said Patty. "So we'll need Mantis to corroborate Thompson's story. Thompson said Mantis and Dorisko were together."

"My experience," said Rick, "suggests Dorisko's going to start talking when he learns Thompson's turned against him."

"I hope that your experience portends a successful interview."

CHAPTER TWENTY-NINE

An officer stepped into the break area and caught Patty's attention. "We've got Dorisko in the interview room," he said.

"Thanks," said Patty. She and Rick bussed their table and walked down the hall. Dorisko was clearly not happy to see them.

"What is it now?" he asked.

Rick and Patty ignored the question and sat down across from their suspect.

"Do you remember your rights?" asked Rick.

Dorisko smiled. "Maybe you should read them to me again."

Rick took the small card out of his pocket and read the prisoner his Miranda rights.

Dorisko shrugged. "Okay, I'll talk to you. I've got nothing to hide."

"We've been given some information about your past," Rick said. "Specifically, your year at Laney College."

Dorisko's face drained of color and he lost his smile. "What about it?" he asked, attempting to regain his composure.

"You and your friends started your criminal careers early."

"So we sold some dope. Everyone I knew was smoking weed and snorting coke."

"We're not talking about everyone," said Rick. "Let's discuss how you and

Suzie Browne spent that year selling dope to college kids. One kid in particular, who didn't want to go along with your plan. She went missing."

"I don't remember anything about that," said Dorisko.

"You tried to recruit a college student who didn't want any part of your business."

"I didn't do the recruiting. Suzie did. You should be talking with her."

"You took the student into the woods and killed her. Then you asked Thompson and Heising to bury her."

Dorisko now showed fear in his eyes. "You're making this up."

"You know we're not, and Vic Thompson will testify to it. He'll testify that you killed that girl."

Dorisko was silent.

"You look like a trapped rat," Rick said. "You'd be pacing the floor and attempting to climb the walls if you could. You killed that girl and then enlisted the help of Thompson and Heising to bury the body. We've got the necklace you took from the girl and gave to Thompson. He's agreed to show us where she's buried. We've got you, Dorisko, and you're never going to see the outside again."

Dorisko sat quietly staring at his hands. Patty and Rick glanced at each other.

"David," Patty said quietly, "you can see where this is going. Mantis has already told us you killed Heising in the storage unit. Now Thompson's ready to testify that you also killed the student from Laney College. The DA will want the death penalty."

Dorisko shook his head. "All I've done for them, and now they turn on me. Well, they're not taking me down. I didn't kill that college girl. Suzie did. The girl threatened to go to the police with information that would have proven Suzie was selling drugs on campus. Suzie told me we had to get rid of the girl. She told me that if the cops picked her up, she'd take me with her. So she got the girl to get high and took her into the woods. Suzie told me that she shot the girl. Later, she showed up at my place and told me what she'd done. I went with her to look at where the body was. Suzie had pulled it off the path and hidden it with leaves. I went back for Thompson and Heising to help bury her."

"Do you have any way of proving it was Suzie and not you who shot the girl?"

"No."

"And Heising?" asked Patty. "Who killed him?"

"I don't know. I didn't even know he was in Brookings."

"Why would Heising want to kill June Deboe?" asked Patty.

Dorisko shook his head again. "Last I heard from Heising, he wanted nothing more to do with the drug scene. I don't know how he knew Deboe."

"This doesn't look good for you, Dorisko," said Patty. "You knew Vic Thompson was planning to kill Suzie Mantis and you did nothing. Now you say that when you all were in college, you knew Mantis was going to kill a student and you did nothing to stop her. If there's anything you're not telling us, we're going to find out. Mantis and Thompson are making a case that will put you away for a very long time."

"They can't prove what they're saying," said Dorisko. "I'm telling you the truth."

When the interview ended, the detectives left the PD for the hospital, where they'd talk again with Suzie Mantis. The patient was awake and watching TV. The detectives stopped at the nurses' station for some information before walking into the room. As Rick walked into the room, he hummed a few lines from the song, *Wake Up Little Suzie*. Patty looked at him and smiled.

"Hello, Suzie," said Patty.

"Hi," she said without taking her eyes away from the TV.

Rick picked up the remote, pointed it at the TV, and hit off.

"Hey," Suzie said. "I was watching that."

"And now you're not," Rick said.

"What do you want now?"

Patty walked toward the head of the bed. "A few things have come to light since we last spoke with you."

"Now what? I told you I sold drugs to June Deboe, but I'm no longer into that scene. Tomorrow, when I'm discharged, I'm going to leave Eugene and go someplace where I can start again. I've already told Tommy that coming this close to death has only confirmed the fact that I want to stay clean, and I don't want to spend my life in a house taking care of other people. I'm going to get a fresh start."

"You'll have a change of lifestyle when you leave here," said Patty, "but it won't be the fresh start you're thinking about."

Suzie smiled. "You've got nothing on me other than my selling some drugs."

"You've got a bad memory," said Patty. "Tell us what you remember about your year at Laney College."

Suzie lost her smile, then panned the room with her eyes. "So I went to college. A lot of kids did."

"A student went missing while you were there, and you know what happened to her."

Patty could see tiny beads of sweat forming on Suzie's forehead. The skin on her face, neck, and arms was turning a light crimson.

"I don't know what you're talking about," said Suzie.

"Well, that's odd. Because Dorisko and Thompson know all about it. They've given you up."

"Dorisko wouldn't do that. And Thompson wasn't there."

"Wasn't there?" asked Patty. "Wasn't where?"

"What did Dorisko say I did?" Suzie asked.

"He told us you killed the student, and then threatened to kill him too if he told anyone."

"Oh, my God. He's a liar. What's he trying to pull?"

"He's trying to save himself, Suzie. Just like we suggested you do the last time we were here."

"He's been threatening Vic and me for fifteen years. He threatened Howard too, and that's why Howard moved to Nevada. He threatened to kill me. All of us if we told anyone about that girl."

"Not what he says, Suzie. And Thompson will back up Dorisko's story. You're going to be tried for murder."

Suzie Mantis started to cry. "No! I'll confess to selling that girl drugs, but I didn't shoot her."

Patty and Rick exchanged a glance.

"How did you know the girl was shot?" asked Patty.

"Dorisko told me," she said. "He said he killed her."

"Vic Thompson is going to take us to where the girl was buried," said Patty. "We'll find the bullet and cartridge and match it to a gun that was registered to you. You're doing yourself no good lying to us."

Suzie said nothing. Tears rolled down her cheeks and she began to sob quietly.

Patty's cell phone rang, and she looked at caller ID. "I'll step out to take this." Once outside the room Patty said hello to Tom Mantis. "Hello, Mr. Mantis."

"Hello, Detective O'Toole. This is a difficult call."

"What can I do for you?" asked Patty.

"Suzie and I are divorcing. I've been packing up her stuff at home, and I've come across something I didn't know she had."

"What's that?"

"It's a gun, Detective. It was in her bottom dresser drawer. I don't want her to get it back. Can I turn it in to you?"

"I'll have an officer out right away to pick it up. Have you handled it?"

"No. I left it right where it is."

"Do you know what kind of gun it is?"

"No, I'm sorry. I really don't know firearms."

"Thanks for calling, Mr. Mantis."

Patty called Strand and asked that an officer pick up the gun. "I'm hoping that the only prints we'll find are those of Suzie Mantis."

"I'll make sure the officer is careful," said Strand. "Do you want to see it before we send it to the lab?"

"Photos will do," said Patty. "I'd appreciate your emailing them to me and then expediting the prints."

"I'll take care of it."

"Thanks, Strand."

Patty called Detective Thursday in Alameda County.

"Detective, this is Detective O'Toole. My partner and I are in Eugene talking with Suzie Browne Mantis, one of the suspects in the death of your missing student. She's admitted to selling drugs to students at the Laney campus, and her husband just called to let me know that he's found a gun belonging to our suspect. We should have prints within twenty-four hours. She's due to be released tomorrow from the hospital, and I believe she's a flight risk."

"I'll call the DA and see how fast he can get a warrant from the judge."

Patty walked back into the room, pulled Rick aside, and let him know about the calls.

"This should change her position," said Rick.

Patty approached the head of Suzie's bed. "I just spoke with your husband."

"Not for long," said Suzie.

"He's been packing up your stuff for you. And cleaning out your dresser."

"My dresser? He knows not to touch the stuff in my dresser. I need to make a phone call."

"Too late, Suzie. He just told me about the gun. We've got an officer on the way to your house now to pick it up. Your prints are on the gun, Suzie, and we're going to match the gun to the bullet and cartridge we find with the body of the girl you shot."

Suzie Mantis threw her head back. "Stupid, stupid," she said. "Okay, okay! The girl told me she didn't want to sell for me anymore. Said she wanted to quit. I'd already told her about the business me and Dorisko set up, and she'd sold on campus for us. She should have known we couldn't let her out. She'd go to the cops and ruin our business and our lives. You know how it is when you're in college. Making money is more important than anything else. And we were making a lot of it. Dorisko and I were living the good life. I couldn't let her take it all away. So I walked with her into the woods and pushed her. She fell to the ground and I shot her." Suzie looked up at Patty and Rick with pleading eyes. "You can understand, can't you? She was going to ruin our lives."

"What did Dorisko have to do with the death?" asked Patty.

"I went back to the campus and told him what I'd done. I showed him where the body was. He told me to go back home and he'd take care of it. Later he told me that Heising and Thompson helped him bury the body."

Patty and Rick left the room. Patty called the lieutenant while Rick gave the officer guarding the room an update of the charges, emphasizing that only medical personnel were allowed in the room.

"Hi, LT, it's Patty. Rick and I have just interviewed Suzie Mantis, and she's confessed to killing the Laney College student. The student was shot with Suzie's gun. An officer is picking up the gun at the Mantis home, and it will be sent to the criminalist lab for fingerprint processing and matching the casings found at our double homicide scene. I'll also have the lab send a casing to Detective Thursday for his use in the event he finds the Laney College student's body. Rick and I will head home tomorrow."

"Good work, O'Toole. Check in with me when you two return."

The detectives drove back to the PD and sat in Strand's office talking before leaving for Brookings.

"She was the last of the three that I'd figured for the responsible," said Rick. "She was married with kids, had a husband who not only supported his family but wanted to. She had everything going for her."

"She didn't have them when she murdered the girl," said Patty. "She probably never considered that her life might change for the better, and most drug users can't see beyond their need."

"From what you two have told me," said Strand, "the kids and husband are a lot better off without her. She's a narcissistic, bad person."

"She is," said Rick. "I arrested a few basically bad people in Boston. They don't know how to care or appreciate others. They're absorbed with themselves."

Patty shook hands with Strand. "Thanks again for your help."

"Before you go," said Strand, "I've been meaning to ask. That Brookings case you had about three years ago, where a serial killer hung a retired cop. Did you ever confirm that he was also responsible for the Arcadia, Louisiana officer?"

Patty looked up at Rick and then back to Strand. "We did, and that was a another forensic feat!" She and Rick walked out of the office.

CHAPTER THIRTY

The next day Patty and Rick drove back to Brookings.

"It will be nice to have more than a couple days at home," said Rick.

"I agree," said Patty. "I'm looking forward to sleeping in my own bed with my own pillow."

"On the case," Rick asked, "which one of our three suspects had reason to want Heising dead?"

"Dorisko may have thought that Heising was interested in the coke hidden in the unit," said Patty.

"He may also have been afraid that Heising was going to the authorities about the Laney College murder," said Rick. "And he may have hired someone like Cooper to get rid of the problem."

"And then there's Suzie Mantis," said Patty. "We know now that she's capable of murder. Why would she have wanted Heising dead?"

"That's something we may never find out," said Rick.

Upon their return to Brookings, Patty went straight home, poured herself a glass of Chardonnay, and sat down in her favorite living room chair. Relaxation was beginning to set in when her phone rang.

"Hi, Mom. How's the trip?"

"Going great, dear. We've been to a couple of private ranches and a private wildlife preserve. I wish you could have seen the baby bears! There were about eight of them, and they were cute as anything we've ever seen."

"What a treat, Mom! What kind of an enclosure were they in?"

"Oh, they had a huge area with a large pool, trees, and lots of running space. They were just like kids in the pool, standing on their hind legs and one bear trying to push another bear over. Then they'd chase each other up and down the trees. Bill and I both got a big kick out of them."

"Seems like a good way to wind up your trip. Are you both ready to come home?"

"Oh, yes. It's great to be away, but home is always a welcome sight. How's your case going?"

"It's getting there. I should be able to tell you more in a few days."

"Okay," said Maggie. "I won't ask for more information now. Bill and I will want you, Becky, and Rick to come over soon after we get back home. You can tell us about the case, and we'll talk more about our trip."

"We'd enjoy that. You'll want to invite Barbara too."

"Oh? Oh, okay. Are you all right?"

"Of course. Why wouldn't I be?"

"Just asking."

"Let me know when your plane lands, Mom, and I'll pick you and Bill up."

"Thanks, dear. I'll call or text tomorrow with the time. Love you."

"Love you too, Mom."

* * *

Patty was at her desk when Rick walked in.

"I think I slept ten hours last night," he said. "I was asleep before my head hit the pillow."

"Yeah," said Patty. "Me too. Mom called, and then I went to bed. She wants you and Barbara to join Becky and me at their place for dinner soon so that they can tell us about their trip."

Rick looked at his desk and then back to Patty. "That's nice." He then exhaled slowly and leaned back in his chair.

"You look like someone just took your last bacon-topped maple bar. Want to talk about it?"

"I spoke with Barbara before I went to bed last night. She doesn't think our relationship will work. She said she doesn't think she could be a detective's wife. She doesn't like not knowing whether I'm going to be home every evening."

"Well," Patty said, "that seems kind of strange. From what you've told me, she often has interruptions in her evenings."

"She knows that and says that two people with unsteady schedules can't make for a good relationship. She said good-bye again."

"I'm sorry, Rick. Sorry you're being hurt again, and I'm sorry for her."

Rick lifted his eyes. "For her?"

"Yes. She's losing out in a relationship with one of the best men I've ever met. You're caring and kind, and one heck of a detective. You're a man with character, and she'll be sorry someday that she didn't snag you when you wanted her. Any woman would be fortunate to have a husband like you."

Patty stared at Rick and he stared back.

"I didn't know you thought that way about me," he said.

"Well, I guess I've never been driven to tell you. I just don't like seeing you hurt."

Rick started to speak but held back. A few seconds passed before he picked up his coffee cup and started drinking. Patty opened a file and continued writing her report.

The detectives spent the rest of their shift putting a dent in the backlog of written reports that were due. At five o'clock Patty stood up and put her jacket on, preparing to go home. Rick set his pencil down.

"Going home?"

"Yeah. I haven't seen much of Becky lately. It will be good to get home before she dives into her homework and wants to be left alone." Patty picked up her purse and placed the strap over her shoulder. "See you tomorrow."

"Patty," Rick said.

Patty stopped and looked at Rick. "Yes?"

"I just want you to know that what you said earlier means a lot to me."

"It's just the truth, Rick."

"Well, you need to know that I think a lot of you too. And I…"

"You what, Rick?"

Rick fidgeted in his chair. "That's all. I have a lot of admiration for you."

"Thanks," said Patty. "You going home now?"

"In a minute," Rick said.

Patty left the office and Rick sat quietly alone at his desk. He folded the file he'd opened and placed it in his desk drawer. He could hear laughter coming from the break room. He turned off the light and walked out of the building for his car. The sky was clear, and he noticed how bright the stars shone. Across the street a young couple held hands on an evening stroll. Rick got into his car and drove to his AA meeting.

* * *

Patty was busy at her desk. Her phone rang and she glanced at caller ID. "Detective Thursday," she greeted him. "You must have found something."

"We have. We've found a body and expect it will be our missing college student."

"Thompson lead you to it?"

"He did. And that's not all we found."

"The bullet?" asked Patty.

"Yes, and the casing."

"The casing?"

"It was placed on top of the victim before she was buried."

"That's unbelievable," said Patty.

"I've sent the bullet and casing to our county lab," said Thursday. "We'll let you know if the casing we found is a match to the one you sent us from the suspect's gun. We've made this a priority at the lab; therefore, we should hear something within a couple of hours. I've also received the arrest warrant. We'll fly tomorrow to pick up Suzie Mantis. I received the warrant based upon her admitting to the murder, but a match between casings would seal the case, and we wouldn't have to be concerned about her retracting her confession. Was she released from the hospital?"

"Not yet," said Patty. "They'll discharge her today. Strand has an officer at the hospital ready to take her into custody upon her release."

"I'll call him," said Thursday, "and let him know we'll extradite her. I'll let you know when the lab results are back."

"Thanks," said Patty.

Rick had arrived while Patty was on the phone. She shared the latest update with him. "I need to let the LT know," she said as she stood. She pointed to a small white bag on Rick's desk. "Your favorite pastry, if interested."

Rick opened the bag and looked in. "Hmmm. A maple bar with a piece of bacon across the top. How did you know?"

Patty left the room and walked down the hall. The lieutenant was on the phone and waved Patty in. She sat down and waited until he'd completed his call.

"You must have an update," he said.

"We do, LT. The body of the Laney College student has been discovered in Alameda County. Vic Thompson took them right to her. She was shot."

"So they have the bullet," said the lieutenant.

Patty nodded. "And the casing!"

"Where'd they find it?"

Detective Thursday said it was lying on top of the body. As though some-one intentionally set it there."

"Have they matched it to the gun found in the Mantis home?"

"Thursday expects to know within a couple of hours."

"And our state lab?"

"It's taking a little longer due, I'm sure, to the fact that Alameda County has a lot more resources that we do. But Oregon's state lab knows this is a priority."

"That's good news, O'Toole. Let me know when you hear from either lab. Tell Rick I'm impressed with the work the two of you have done."

"I'll do that," said Patty. "Thanks." She walked back to her desk. "It's kind of funny."

"What's that?" asked Rick.

"That someone may have thrown the casing in on top of the body in order to keep anyone from finding it on the ground. It's the ultimate piece of evidence."

"Investigating crimes in Boston I learned that most criminals do stupid things," said Rick. "Nothing surprises me anymore."

An hour had passed when Patty's phone rang. "It's Thursday," she said to Rick.

Rick put his pencil down, and Patty put the phone on speaker.

"Detective Thursday," Patty greeted him.

"Hi, O'Toole. Our lab criminalists just called me. The casing found with the body of our missing college student matches the casing you sent over from the gun owned by Suzie Mantis. We now have evidence that supports her confession."

"That's great," said Patty. "Starker's here so I've got you on speaker."

"Thanks to you both," said Thursday. "Knowing the responsible is going to spend the rest of her life in prison will be helpful information to the bereaved parents."

"I agree," said Rick. "Glad we could help."

"I'll let you know the lab results here when we have them," said Patty.

"Thanks," said Thursday. "Hope it solves your case."

The call ended, and Patty walked down the hall to give the lieutenant Thursday's results.

She returned to her desk to find Rick staring out the window. "You look to be studying something. Thinking about the case?"

Rick turned back to his desk. "No, just noticing the sunny day outside."

"We're supposed to have twenty-five-foot waves today, due to some storm off the coast. Why don't we get a couple of deli sandwiches for lunch, sit in our car, and be entertained by the waves breaking up against our sea stacks?"

"Yeah. That's a good idea. I'll use the time until then answering a couple of calls and finishing another report."

"I've got work to do too," said Patty.

Two hours later, the detectives were preparing to leave for lunch when Patty received the anticipated call from the Oregon state lab. She got Rick's attention and put the call on speaker.

"Detective O'Toole."

"Good morning, Detective. This is Sam from the criminalist division of the Oregon State lab. How's your day going?"

Patty smiled. "Starker and I are having a pretty good day here, Sam. I've got you on speaker so that he can hear what I hope is good news."

"Well," said Sam, "if you'd told me the day wasn't going well, I'd have said that I'm about to make it a lot better. The fingerprints on the gun are those of Suzie Mantis, and the casing you sent to us from her gun is a match to the 9mm casing found in the storage unit. I believe you've got your responsible."

Rick and Patty both smiled and looked at each other. "That's great news, Sam," said Patty. "You've definitely made our day."

"That's what I live for. You two stay safe out there."

"Thanks, Sam," said Rick.

"No problem."

Patty gave the news to her lieutenant, who paused before speaking. "Let Strand know we can't extradite her as planned," he said. "We'll need her to stand trial for the murder of Howard Heising. Alameda County can then process her for the murder of the Laney College student."

"I'll let him know," said Patty.

"O'Toole," said the lieutenant.

"Yes?"

"Great work on the part of you and Rick. I knew you two could solve this. You make a great team."

"Thanks, LT. I'll pass that on to Rick."

EPILOGUE

Six weeks later, Rick and Patty were at their desks preparing for the day.

"I can't get over," said Patty, "how Suzie Mantis was able to manipulate Heising into killing June Deboe as part of a plan to eliminate them both."

"She said Heising was in love with her," said Rick. "She told him that if June went to the authorities, it would ruin their chances together. I have no doubt that Heising didn't fully understand what he was getting into with Mantis."

"She's a true sociopath," said Patty. "No feelings for anyone other than herself."

"Speaking bluntly," said Rick, "she's a cold-blooded killer."

They both sat quietly for a minute.

"Patty," Rick said, "there's something I want to tell you."

Patty looked up from her desk. "Yes?"

"A couple of months ago I put in for a job with the Oregon state DOJ. They need an experienced detective for their homicide division."

"An agent for the DOJ? You'd have to move to Salem."

"I know. Yesterday I received a response in the mail. They've offered me the position."

Patty's eyes filled with tears. "Are you seriously considering leaving?"

Rick locked eyes with her and didn't respond.

"Why?" she asked.

"A couple of reasons," said Rick. "There's a huge salary increase for one."

"And the second?"

"It's been eight years now since Claire and Skylar died. I can never replace them in my life, but I'm ready to settle down with someone. I realized after this last attempt to make things work with Barbara that it's futile for me to think she'd ever be willing to accept me and my job. I'm thinking that this position with the DOJ will give me a fresh start."

Patty was silent as she wiped the tears from her eyes. "Are you going to spend some time thinking about it?"

"I have, Patty. I start next month."

My readers are important to me, and for them I write a quarterly newsletter. It's easy to receive if you're interested. Just log on to my website, https://www.colorandwordsbygeorgia.com. Click on *Contact Me* and ask to receive the newsletter. You can also send me an email at colorandwordsbygeorgia@gmail.com should you have questions or comments.

May I ask something of you? If you liked *Murder Takes All*, please go to Amazon.com, bring up my book on the search screen, and leave a review. Your kind words are always appreciated.

MURDER REPLETE...*for now*

Book Three in the O'Toole/Starker Oregon Coast murder mystery series.

A man found hanging in a usually serene Oregon forest sends the town of Brookings into a panic and brings Detectives Patty O'Toole and Rick Starker running. Who is he? What has he done to be murdered in such a way? Uncovering the answers proves to be more complex than they first expect. The man's past looks like a promising lead, but no sooner do they discover possible motives in his history when they learn of another death. Do the similarities lead back to the same twisted mind? As the body count mounts, the detectives realize that they could be dealing with their very first serial killer. One who is always watching.

ABOUT G. A. COCKERHAM

G. A. Cockerham lives on the southern Oregon coast, the inspiration for her O'Toole/Starker murder mystery series. She is a retired investment advisor and insurance broker.
colorandwordsbygeorgia@gmail.com

Made in the USA
Middletown, DE
22 June 2020